D1607542

MacMillan Wharf

Richard Gifford

ISBN:1453796231
ISBN-13: 978-1453796238

TO NANCY, BEN AND JACK

ACKNOWLEDGMENTS

Thanks to all who encouraged me in the writing of this story. To my son Benjamin, for whom without regular naptimes this story would not have been written. For my son Jack, who appreciates a good story. Most of all thanks to my wife Nancy, without whose constant patience and support I would be adrift.

This book is dedicated to the memory of John Prophet, for his editing skills and encouragement.

Cover photo: Christopher Seufert

i

Chapter 1

"If you look off of the starboard bow, you'll see a humpback whale named Stormy and her calf, Squall" said Annie Macalister. One hundred and twenty-seven tourists leaned against the railing. The ninety foot whale watch boat Explorer heeled over to one side so that they could all snap spectacular pictures that would later appear as nothing more than a vast expanse of ocean with two barely discernible, wet black lumps above the water. Fourth of July weekend was always busy in Provincetown, and the Explorer was nearly filled to capacity with visitors looking to escape the oppressive heat back on land.

This was Annie's fourth trip of the day out of Provincetown. There were so many things running through her mind that the whale sightings just seemed routine. Annie had seen scores of whales since she arrived in May. Not just the entertaining humpbacks with their acrobatics and curiosity, but finbacks, minkes, pilot whales and porpoises by the hundreds. Annie's most exciting day was when she caught a glimpse of a North Atlantic Right Whale, the most endangered cetacean in the world.

This summer, she was interning at the Whale Center in Provincetown, which meant that she was out on the boat six days a week, four trips each day. In the mornings, she would help out at the center, sometimes answering phones or filing reports, but her favorite job was working alongside Dr. Linda Hanscomb who knew more about the demise of the right whale than any other living person.

In just a few weeks, she will have to move out of her tiny room off Commercial Street and cram everything she owned into her battered 1992 Honda Civic, then drive ten hours back to her final year at the College of the Atlantic in Bar Harbor, Maine where she majors in Human Ecology.

"Whatever the hell that is," as her father is fond of saying. She's tried to explain to him many times that she is interested in studying whales, and that you can't possibly study whales without understanding the history and economics of the whaling industry, both past and present. Annie doubted that he would ever understand. It would be easier after graduate school, she hoped, when she could just say that she is a marine biologist.

Annie felt sad about leaving Provincetown at the end of the summer. When she arrived in May she didn't know what to make of this quirky, beautiful town at the end of Cape Cod. A hodgepodge of artists, scientists, fishermen and shopkeepers, Provincetown had become the best known gay vacation spot on the East Coast. Annie was at first surprised at the openness on the streets, but she was used to it now, even comfortable with it.

When she told her parents that she was going to spend the summer in P-Town, they immediately became suspicious. Her father Roy just sighed "Jesus Christ" and went back to his newspaper in the den.

Her mother Martha said, "Oh that sounds nice dear" and hurriedly cleared the dishes from the dinner table. Later, over coffee, she quietly said to Annie, "You know I love you no matter what you are, but if you think you are gay, I don't think you should tell Dad, you know how he is." Annie assured her mother that she wasn't a lesbian. Just the spoken word made Martha wince. Annie didn't want to tell her about her boyfriend Shane who owned a lobster boat and his own house, but he could certainly testify that what she said was true.

The scream from the stern snapped Annie out of her daydream. A nasally New Yorker was shrieking "Ohmygod! There's a body in the watah!" There was a scramble on the bridge as Annie and Captain Billy Souza grabbed for the yellow Nikon binoculars at the same time. Annie learned over the summer that she may know a little bit about whales, but this was sure as hell Capt. Billy's boat. He grabbed the binoculars and scanned the water. Below them, two dozen sunburned arms were pointing to the same object bobbing in the waves.

"Shit", Billy muttered. He could see the body floating face down about fifty yards off the port stern. He took the boat out of neutral, where they had been idling to allow everyone a look at the whales, and nudged the throttle into forward. The twin Caterpillar diesels snorted awake, and using the bow thruster, Billy spun the ninety foot vessel around in its own length. "Annie, Juicy, grab some boat hooks and get down to the stern," he shouted over the noise of the engines.

"Yah, mon," said Juicy Freeman in his lilting Jamaican accent. He moved with a great deal more urgency than Annie had ever seen before.

Nervously, Annie hurried down the two flights of stairs to the stern with Juicy. As the big boat inched up on the body, Annie could see that it was bound with rope at the wrists and ankles.

"Hold it!" Juicy yelled over the diesels while putting one hand in the air with the universal signal to stop.

Capt. Billy put both engines in neutral and let the momentum of the boat close the final few feet, so that the two could snag the body.

Annie's stomach churned in knots as she reached out with the boat hook. She missed and splashed the water, but Juicy's hook caught the rope binding the corpse's feet. As he pulled the body in, Juicy passed his boat hook to Annie so that he could grab the back of the shirt and heave the body onto the deck. In one swift motion, he pulled the body out of the water. It dropped onto the steel deck with a sickening, wet thud that echoed through the hull.

Annie couldn't believe what she saw. At her feet was a woman's body. Her long blonde hair was matted with seaweed and her lifeless pale blue eyes stared into Annie's. She felt queasy and light-headed, as if she were going to faint. Her eyes rolled back into

4

her head and Annie's entire body went limp. Juicy must have seen the look in her face as he caught Annie before she collapsed. He laid her down gently next to the body of Dr. Linda Hanscomb.

Chapter 2

Provincetown Police Chief Tony Souza's phone rang just as he was about to take a bite of what once was hot kale soup that he picked up from the Portuguese Bakery on Commercial Street three hours earlier. It was his direct line. "This is Chief Souza".

"Dad, it's Billy" said the familiar voice on the other end of the phone. "We're about two miles off Race Point, and we're heading in early. Some of the passengers spotted a body floating in the water. Juicy and Annie managed to haul it on board. It looks like Linda Hanscomb from the Whale Center."

The Chief sat up straight in his vinyl swivel chair, grabbed a pen, and started writing furiously on the legal pad that he always kept on his desk. "OK, Billy, how long until you're back?"

"I'm running flat out at just under forty knots, so I should be at the dock in half an hour." Captain Billy shouted over the hum of the twin six hundred horsepower diesels.

"Alright, I'll meet you there. Have you called the Coast Guard yet?"

"No."

"I'll let them know then. I'm sure there will be some paperwork for you to fill out"

"OK, dad, I'll see you soon. Bye."

Chief Souza didn't have a chance to reply. There was too much that needed to happen. He opened his door and walked over to Officer Carla Thompson, the dispatcher and only other person in the station, and told her what was going on. Carla called the Provincetown Fire Department to request an ambulance, the Coast Guard to report a death at sea, and the district attorney's office in

Barnstable. She also radioed for all available officers to meet the Explorer when it arrived at its berth.

The Chief jogged out the door to his Crown Victoria. He slipped behind the wheel and started the engine. Dropping the transmission into reverse, he flipped on the lights and siren, pulled onto Shankpainter Road, and made his way to MacMillan Wharf to meet his son, Annie, Juicy, one hundred twenty-seven distraught passengers, and the body of Linda Hanscomb.

Anthony "Tony" James Souza was born in the winter of 1952 in his parent's home on Bradford Street in Provincetown where he still lived. At the time, Provincetown was primarily a Portuguese and Cape Verdean fishing port with an active artists' colony in the summer. Everyone got along pretty well, although times were much harder then. In 1970, Billy was inducted into the United States Army and was sent to Vietnam. He saw enough bloodshed in two years to last a lifetime.

When he returned from the war, he joined his brother John on the fishing boat that they inherited from their father Pasquale. John and Tony fished together for a year and a half, but Tony never got his fair share of the profits, and felt that he did more than half the work. After one nasty disagreement that ended in a fist fight six miles off shore, Tony quit fishing and joined the Provincetown Police. John still lived and fished in Provincetown, and when they saw each other around town, they simply nodded to one another, but only exchanged words on rare occasions.

He was barely on the force for three months when he was called to the scene of his first murder. In the summer of 1974, the entire region was shocked by the case of what has come to be known as "the lady of the dunes".

After thirty years, this case still haunted him. A woman was found with both hands severed. No one ever reported her missing or claimed the body. No name, no next of kin, no suspects, nothing. It was as if she had never existed, but Tony Souza knew indeed that she had. The woman's lifeless face was permanently etched into his mind.

Every time he heard about an unsolved murder within a hundred miles, Chief Souza wondered if the same killer had struck again. He always had a suspicion that the lady of the dunes' killer was a local.

As he crossed over Commercial Street, his car was enveloped in the colorful chaos that marks the Fourth of July weekend in Provincetown; shirtless bodybuilders with tattoos and piercings, male and female couples walking hand in hand, gawking tourists, overtired kids, drag queens on scooters, and all the usual sights and sounds of this unusual place.

He could see that the ambulance had just arrived at the Explorer's pier on MacMillan Wharf. Two of his bicycle officers were already on scene. "That's the best way to get around here in the summer" the chief thought to himself. "How the hell did she get here so fast?" he said aloud.

Leaning against the Explorer's ticket booth was the familiar sight of Betsy Gilmore, Provincetown reporter for the Cape Cod Telegraph.

The chief shifted the car into park and turned off the engine, but left the flashing blue strobe lights on. A crowd had already gathered while the boat had yet to round Long Point, the entrance to Provincetown Harbor. He stepped out of the car, swept his silver hair back with his left hand and placed his mesh summer cap on with his right. Betsy Gilmore was already moving towards him like a hyena stalking its prey.

"Hi ,Chief, what's going on?" asked Betsy. "I heard on the scanner that the Explorer found a body at sea. Do you know anything else?"

"Sorry Betsy, that's all I know right now. I've got a lot of work to do here, so if you'll excuse me…" Chief Souza tried to brush past her, but Betsy managed to step in front of him in the crowd.

"Sure Chief, just one quick question. Isn't your son Billy captain of the Explorer?"

"Yes he is." Chief Souza was very proud of his son. After graduating from Provincetown High School second in a class of 32, Billy enrolled at the Massachusetts Maritime Academy in Buzzards Bay where he earned a degree in marine engineering. He also earned his 100-ton captains' license. "Little Billy", as he was known to the family, was hired as Captain of the Explorer one year ago at the age of 23.

"OK, thanks Chief," said Betsy. "Will there be a press briefing later?"

"I'll let you know. Now if you'll excuse me…" he said as he walked away.

Pain in the ass reporters, Chief Souza thought. Always trying to get a story before they have the facts.

Officers Matt Costa and Cheryl McGuire were chatting with the EMT's in front of the Explorer's ramp. Their Trek police mountain bikes were perched on their kickstands on either side of the ramp. With the battery-powered strobe lights on, they made for an effective barrier to hold back the growing crowd.

"What's going on Chief?" asked Matt.

Matt and his son Billy were friends growing up and played football together at Provincetown High School. Matt applied for a summer officer position last year while working on his associate degree in Criminal Justice at Cape Cod Community College. Chief Souza immediately hired him and kept him on year round.

"Billy called me and said that they found a body floating off shore. He thinks it might be one of the scientists over at the Whale

Center," the Chief responded in a low voice.

"Was it an accident?" asked Officer McGuire.

"Don't know" said the chief. He knew from experience that he needed to be careful when stating unsubstantiated facts, even to his own officers. People like to make assumptions and quick judgments, but Chief Souza knew that real life is usually far more complicated.

"Here comes the boat" said Carol Anderson, a compact, powerful woman who, in addition to being an EMT, was a competitive triathlete. She moved to Provincetown two years ago to live and train with her partner Susan, who she met while competing in local triathlons around New England. The two could be seen biking, running, or swimming together throughout the year.

"All right," said the chief, "when the boat docks, we'll let the passengers off first, then we'll take the body. Let's try not to let this become a circus."

Between the crowds, Betsy Gilmore, who had now been joined by a photographer, the flashing red, white and blue lights on the ambulance, the lights on his car, and the bicycles, Chief Souza glanced around and knew that it was too late.

Chapter 3

The ninety-foot white hull of the Explorer inched up to the dock. The deckhands secured the bow and stern lines to the large cleats on the floating platform. Once the boat was tied off, Captain Billy cut the engines and Juicy stepped down to the dock to wheel over the aluminum gangway.

The passengers pushed and shoved their way to the gangway like nervous cattle. Spending half an hour with a murdered woman was enough to ruin any thoughts of ice cream and foot-long hot dogs that awaited their return to dry land. As the last passenger disembarked, Chief Souza and his small entourage of officers and EMTs strode up the walkway and onto the boat.

Annie sat in the wheelhouse next to Captain Billy, who had been very kind to her since he realized that the body was that of her friend and mentor. Billy admired Annie's good looks, bright smile, and sense of humor from the first time they met. He knew her boyfriend, Shane, from around town, but he didn't know Annie well enough to tell her that she could do better. For the past month, he waited for them to break up so that he might ask her out, but that never happened. Now, he had a chance to show her his kinder side.

Once the engine stopped, Billy turned to Annie and asked "you okay?"

"I guess so," Annie lied.

"I need to go down and talk to them," he nodded his head towards the police and rescue workers standing in a circle around Linda Hanscomb's corpse, "You want to come or wait here?"

Her voice was barely above a whisper. "I'll stay here for now. I don't want to see her like that again."

Annie had come to respect and admire Linda's work this

summer. Not only was she a skilled researcher and advocate for the whales, she was also a kind and patient teacher who had become a close friend. Clearly, Linda had been murdered. Why would anyone want to do such a thing? Annie vowed to herself that she would try to find the answer.

Billy headed down the aluminum stairs to the stern of ship where Dr. Hanscomb's body lay covered by two orange foul weather coats. He watched as his father pulled back the hood of the coat that covered her face. The others officers stepped back from the grisly scene.

Who would do this? the chief wondered. Somebody wanted her gone, and judging by where she was found, the body was probably dumped from a boat well off shore.

"Hi Dad," Billy mumbled as he stepped into the gathered circle. He always felt funny calling the chief of police "Dad" in public. "What do think happened?"

"It's hard to say at this point. We'll have to wait for an autopsy. Where did you say you found her?"

"About two miles off of Race Point. We'd been watching a mother and calf humpback for a while, and a passenger spotted the body floating."

"Did you find anything else when you pulled her out of the water?"

"No, she was just like she is now. When Juicy and Annie brought her on board, I had them leave her right here. I asked Juicy to cover her with something so the passengers wouldn't be any more upset than they already were. Annie is taking it pretty hard. She was close with Linda. Linda'd been out on a few trips with me earlier in the season so I recognized her right away."

The chief paused for a moment, then asked, "Is Annie still here?"

"Yeah, she's up in the wheelhouse."

"I need to talk to her."

As the father and son Souzas headed up to the wheelhouse, Officers Costa and McGuire watched the two Provincetown EMTs gently lift Linda's body onto a gurney then zip her into a black body bag.

Annie watched from the wheelhouse as they rolled the gurney down the ramp to the dock where the ambulance was parked on the wharf. Her chin quivered, but she was still in too much shock to cry.

She was startled when she heard Billy's voice behind her. "Annie, have you met my father, Chief Souza?"

"Hello Annie, I'm Chief Souza with the Provincetown Police Department" the elder Souza said as he removed his hat and extended his hand. "I'm sorry about Dr. Hanscomb. Billy tells me that you two were close."

"I work with her, and she's my friend," said Annie not yet being able to refer to Linda in the past tense.

"When was the last time you saw her?" asked Chief Souza in a gentle, sympathetic tone.

"Last night, about eight-thirty. When we got back from our last trip, I stopped by the center to check the schedule for next week. I saw Linda in her office and we chatted for a few minutes."

"What did you talk about?"

"Nothing much, just small talk, really. We made plans to go out this weekend for dinner with her girlfriend, Mary Ellen." The look on her face changed instantly from sadness to panic. "Oh God! Mary Ellen. Has anyone called her? I've got to call her."

"Who?"

"Mary Ellen Johnson"

"Would she be next of kin?" asked the chief.

"I guess so," Annie replied, "they've been living here together for a few years. She owns a gallery called Dharma in the East End, she's probably there now."

Chief Souza paused for a minute and looked out the front window. He could see the EMTs loading Linda's body into the ambulance. He watched as the photographer from the Cape Cod Telegraph ran around snapping pictures from every angle he could, while Betsy Gilmore scribbled furiously in her notebook. "Friggin' vultures", he muttered. He knew that more would be coming soon. They were probably on their way from Boston already with satellite trucks. Bad news travels fast, he thought.

"Okay Annie, why don't you go home and get some rest. You've had a hard day," said Chief Souza.

"But what about Mary Ellen? Somebody needs to tell her"

"I'll head over there right now. Do you want a ride home? I can have a car drop you off."

"I'm coming with you" said Annie adamantly. "Linda was my friend and Mary Ellen is, too."

"I don't think that's a good idea."

"C'mon Annie, I'll drive you home," said Billy sheepishly.

"Listen, you two, I have to tell Mary Ellen right now. With all the people on Commercial Street, I can run there faster than you can drive."

Chief Souza knew that she was right. If Annie worked and socialized with the deceased, then she might be useful on this case.

"Okay, let's go" he conceded. The three left the wheelhouse and started up the ramp to MacMillan Wharf.

Chapter 4

Annie was the first to spot Mary Ellen running up to the ambulance in bare feet, carrying a brown leather sandal in each hand. Strands of her curly brown hair were stuck to her face with sweat. She was gasping for breath both from crying and sprinting from her gallery to the wharf in the late afternoon heat.

"Linda!" she cried out, "Linda!" She ran to the closed door of the ambulance and pounded on the glass with her fists. By the time Annie reached her, Mary Ellen could see the knowing look of anguish on her face, and she immediately collapsed into Annie's arms wailing, "Oh God, Annie, tell me it's not true" Mary Ellen demanded.

Annie didn't know what to say, so she said nothing and just held Mary Ellen closer.

"Someone came into the gallery" said Mary Ellen, "and he told me that the Explorer found a body off shore and that it was someone from the Whale Center. I tried to call Linda at her office, but they said she hadn't come in, so I tried her cell phone and there was no answer. That's not like her, Annie. I just knew that something was wrong. When I saw the ambulance, I felt sick, and I knew it was her. Oh God, what happened?"

"I don't know," said Annie. "But it wasn't an accident."

Chief Souza was stood next to them, listening intently to what Mary Ellen and Annie were saying. He didn't want to miss any clue that could point him in the right direction. He was amazed at how quickly word spread around town about what was going on at MacMillan Wharf.

The chief introduced himself. "I'm Chief Souza with the Provincetown Police. Annie said that you knew the deceased?"

"Yes, Linda and I have lived together for almost five years. We were going to get married this fall, once the season was over," replied a sobbing Mary Ellen.

Chief Souza still wasn't used to the idea of same sex couples getting married. He wondered what his wife, Barbara, would think of it. Billy was still in high school when she passed away from breast cancer. He and Barbara grew up together in Provincetown, fell in love in high school, and married at St. James the Fisherman Catholic Church when he came back from Vietnam. He knew what it was like to lose the person you are closest to, and he understood the pain and confusion that Mary Ellen must be feeling now. He also knew the feeling of loneliness that she would have to live with in the months and years to come.

"I know this is all very sudden, but it's important that I get some information from both of you before too much time passes," said Chief Souza. "Would you mind coming back to the station with me so we can figure out what happened here?"

"Whatever I can do to help find the bastard who did this to Linda" Mary Ellen seethed under her breath. Changing her tone, she said in her sweet southern drawl, "just one thing, can I see her before they take her away?"

The Chief thought about this for a moment. He remembered how he held Barbara in his arms for nearly an hour after she died. He never wanted to let her go, who would? "Of course," he said quietly. "But I have to warn you, her body has been in the water for some time. She won't look like you expect." He nodded to the EMTs, and the heavy door of the ambulance was opened so that Mary Ellen could spend a few final moments with Linda.

Ted Fernandes, a Provincetown EMT for 12 years, extended a meaty hand to assist Mary Ellen into the back. When she was inside, he respectfully closed the door behind her so that she could have some privacy from the throng of people who had now gathered around the scene.

Once inside, Mary Ellen's world became very small and all she could hear was the idling ambulance engine and the rapid beating of her heart. Her trembling hands reached out to unzip the body bag. She gasped in horror when she first looked at Linda's bloated face. Linda lay there with her eyes closed, almost like she was sunbathing on Herring Cove beach. But, instead of the usual reddish tan she had in the summer, Linda's skin was a languid grey-blue and she had seaweed matted in her hair. Mary Ellen reached out tentatively to touch Linda's face, and was surprised by how cold she felt, like one of the Inuit stone carvings that she features at her gallery.

She sat down on the bench seat and whispered, "Oh sweetheart, who did this to you? Why? Who could ever want to hurt you?" Mary Ellen half expected a reply, but she knew that she was really asking these questions of herself, and that Linda couldn't answer. Instead she just sat there in the metallic womb of the ambulance, holding onto the one thing in her life that she could never let go. The initial shock of seeing Linda quickly turned to grief, she closed her eyes and began to sob.

Mary Ellen Johnson had become accustomed to loss in her life. Growing up in poverty in Georgia, she was only nine when her mother committed suicide by overdosing on sleeping pills, and Mary Ellen was left to care for her abusive, alcoholic father and two younger twin brothers. She was forced to take care of all three of them and took over the cooking and cleaning while her father worked at the Macon County Correctional Facility. After abusing inmates all day, he would often stop off at a roadside bar on the way home for a few hours. Mary Ellen never knew what kind of mood he would be in when he got home, sometimes he would be the happy drunk and bring presents for the boys and some money for her. Other times he would be like a whirlwind of destruction, wrecking anything or anyone in his path.

The last time Mary Ellen saw her father was nearly twenty

years ago. She was barely fourteen and was just entering high school. The twin boys were in seventh grade. It was a hot and humid Georgia night and she had just finished the evening dishes. By that time she had no idea when her father might come home and really didn't care if he ever did. She decided to take a cool shower since the air conditioning had been broken for two years.

Mary Ellen heard the screen door slam as she was shampooing her hair. Then she heard the bathroom door open. "Hey, I'm in the shower, get out," she yelled, assuming it was one of the pesky twins. She was shocked to hear her father's voice booming "Don't tell me to get out of my own house, girl!" He tore the shower curtain down as he reached out to grab her.

The next few seconds of her life were a chaotic swirl of fists, blood, and profanity. Fortunately, her father slipped on the wet floor and hit his head on the edge of the ragged Formica countertop, causing a huge gash on his forehead. He laid there on the tile unconscious and bleeding. Mary Ellen didn't know if he was alive. She hoped he wasn't. It didn't matter anyway, she was never coming back. She threw on some clothes, grabbed the stash of money she had saved out of the flour container and told the twins that they needed to leave right away.

When Mary Ellen called an aunt in Florida and told her what happened, she immediately drove up to Georgia and took the three back to her home in Gainesville. None of the children ever heard from their father again.

A soft rapping on the door of the ambulance shook Mary Ellen out of her grief.

"Mary Ellen, it's me, Annie." Annie opened the door just enough to peek in. "The chief says we need to go." Annie caught sight of Linda's bloated face and felt her stomach turn into a knot. "I'm so sorry," she said as she gently closed the door.

"I'll be right there Annie." In a whisper she said, "Honey,

I'll always love you, and I will not rest until I find who did this to you. And I'll make them pay. Goodbye sweetie."

Mary Ellen turned and opened the rear door of the ambulance. The bright late afternoon sun blinded her. She felt Annie's hand reach up and take hers to help her down the step. As her eyes adjusted, she could see a huge crowd of people staring at her with a look of pity and confusion.

Betsy Gilmore and her photographer darted out of the crowd. Shoving a tape recorder right into Mary Ellen's face she asked, "Do you have any idea who did this? Are you her lover?" Mary Ellen looked bewildered as the photographer snapped three automatic frames.

"Get the hell away from her!" Annie shouted. "What's wrong with you?"

"Hey, don't try to interfere with the press," Betsy snapped back.

"Alright, leave her alone," the chief said as he jumped between them. Turning to Annie he growled under his breath, "Get her in the car, now."

Annie guided Mary Ellen to the chief's light blue Crown Victoria and held the door for her. By the time she got in, the chief was already in the front seat starting the engine.

"Get us out of here," Annie said. She could see Betsy Gilmore and her photographer elbowing through the crowd to get a better picture.

"I'm trying" said the chief as he turned on the siren. Officers Costa and McGuire pushed the crowd back to give him enough room to turn around. Once he did, he sped across Commercial Street and headed for the police station. "Annie, Ms. Johnson, I know that this is really hard time for you both right now, but I think it would be best if you came to the station with me."

"Chief, I don't know what's going on, but whoever killed Linda is still out there, and probably close by. I don't want him to get away," said Mary Ellen.

"Me neither" said Annie.

That makes three of us, Chief Souza thought to himself.

Chapter 5

Angus Black had good reason to be worried. As CEO of Scotia Gas, his business had expanded rapidly over the previous decade, as had the environmental opposition to offshore oil and gas exploration. The geology of the Gulf of Maine suggests that natural gas reserves exist not just off of Nova Scotia, but all the way to the famed George's Bank fishing grounds. Both Canada and the United States own sides of George's Bank and the disputes over fishing on the Bank have gone on for decades, at times involving gunfire and the intervention of Naval ships from both nations.

Due to the richness of biodiversity on George's Bank, Canada and the United States agreed to a moratorium on oil and gas exploration in the early 1990's. Dolphins, whales, swordfish, lobsters and many other high profile species are found there in abundance. Pressure from fisheries and conservation groups led to both countries protecting the 10,000 square mile underwater plateau from petroleum-related exploration.

However, the moratorium recently expired. The United States still has a ban on oil and gas exploration on George's Bank, but not Canada. Angus Black had made certain through his connections in Ottawa that Scotia Gas was already well-positioned for the exploration rights on the Canadian side of the Bank, but would not be able to gain access to the two-thirds of George's Bank owned by the Americans.

Angus invited a Washington D.C. based oil industry lobbyist named Lloyd "Mac" MacDonald to join him in the hotel bar one evening after the plenary meeting at a recent North-American Petroleum Council conference in Houston, Texas. Angus was dressed neatly in a crisp blue pinstripe Brooks Brothers suit with a white French-cuff shirt and a conservatively striped silk necktie. His gold cufflinks were embossed with the insignia of the British SAS, the special forces unit that he served in as a young man.

He had never married or had children, and rose up the corporate ladder quite quickly as a result.

Mac MacDonald wore his trademark cowboy boots and a bolo tie with an oil rig clasp, all topped off by a large white cowboy hat. Mac was an assistant Secretary of the Interior during the second Reagan administration, and knew the inside track in Washington, DC intimately. Angus knew that Mac was working for some of the large American oil and gas companies, who were just as eager as he was to see drilling on George's Bank. Angus also knew that as long as he kept pouring the liquor, Mac would keep talking. After a few glasses of peaty Islay single malt whiskey, Mac started to open up.

"I'll tell you what Angus, we all know there's a hell of a lot of gas and oil out there. I'm sure it's just a matter of time until the U.S. opens up our side of George's Bank for drilling. Right now the damn Arabs have us by the balls." Mac said in his Texan drawl. "It's just not right that you've got some of the worst regimes in the world in charge of the whole shooting match."

Angus nodded in agreement and refilled Mac's glass with Scotch.

"The problem is going to be with the damn environmental impact reports. These things can take years, and depending on the findings, stop any oil exploration from happening at all."

"And there's no way around it?" Angus asked. He was known in the oil business as being willing to do whatever it took to get his way.

"Not under current law. Hell, Alaska's been held up for nearly a decade because the bunny kissers are all worried that the polar bears might not like the looks of an oil rig." Mac paused to take another sip. "I'll tell you what, I think it will be worse on George's Bank."

"Worse? How?" Angus was well aware of the power of the U.S. Endangered Species Act to stop a project in its tracks.

"Whales." Mac replied dryly.

"Whales? What about them?"

"They're going to be the sticking point, I guarantee it."

"But we have the same whales in Canada, and it wasn't a problem at all."

"You also had the entire province of Nova Scotia going bankrupt after the fishing industry collapsed. How many jobs have you created since exploration opened up on your side?"

"True." Angus saw his point and thought about the thousands of men and women employed by his company and the other supporting industries. The shipyard in Dartmouth, Nova Scotia was running around the clock building new offshore gas rigs. With drilling rights on the American side, his revenues would at least double.

"George's Bank is right next to one of the poorest parts of Canada, but close to the richest parts of the USA. Every year there's hundreds of thousands of people going whale watching, and them whales just tug at people's hearts." Mac elaborated.

A plan was beginning to form in Angus' mind. If he knew what was going to be in the environmental impact statement, he could prepare counter arguments. He could demonstrate that Scotia Gas was already protecting the whale habitats on the Canadian side of George's Bank. Scotia Gas was the largest and most experienced company in the gas industry, and would be well positioned for the American contracts.

"So this environmental impact statement, who's doing it?" Angus asked.

"Some rinky-dink operation in Massachusetts called the Whale Center. That should give you an idea where they're coming from." Mac chuckled. "As far as I understand, they're in charge of collecting all the biological data on the whales' feeding grounds. You see, that's their main concern. The increase in ship traffic and exploration might disturb the whales, and they're all protected by the Endangered Species Act, which doesn't allow that."

Angus had all the information that he thought Mac could be useful for before becoming annoyingly drunk. Checking his Rolex watch, he stood to leave.

"It's always a pleasure chatting with you Mac. I need to catch an early flight in the morning, so I'm heading up to my suite."

"Oh sure thing, compadre. You mind if I finish the bottle?"

"Go right ahead." Angus shook Mac's hand and walked purposefully out of the bar.

When Angus returned to his comfortable office in Halifax from the conference, he turned on his computer and called up the homepage of the Whale Center. He had only recently acquired a computer at home but was rapidly becoming a devotee of the internet. Mostly he used it for on-line auctions of fine art and wine. Now he was learning the usefulness of the internet for prodding around in other people's lives from the comfort of his $800 Herman Miller chair.

The home page of the Whale Center had an employee directory with the friendly and inviting title of "Who We Are." It was complete with pictures, biographies, credentials, and current research projects of each of the staff and interns. One project title in particular caught his interest, "Ecological Degradation of George's Bank by Petroleum Exploration." It only took him a few minutes to find the names and pictures of the authors of the report, Dr. Linda Hanscomb and her assistant Annie Macalister.

He remembered meeting a man from Provincetown at a conference on promoting fisheries and other marine businesses a few years back in Boston who might be able to help get a copy of this report. He dug out his notes from the conference, and found the man's name and phone number circled on the list of attendees. With a simple phone call, and the offer of $5000 for the report, the deal was made.

Chapter 6

Annie, Mary Ellen and the chief were all silent as the police car sped up Bradford Street. As they passed the high school at the top of the hill, Annie had the presence of mind to ask, "Where are we going?"

"I'm taking you two back to the police station. The whole town is going to be crawling with reporters pretty soon and I need to talk to each of you about what happened to Linda."

Mary Ellen stared blankly out the side window of the big car as the little shingled houses passed by. Not in her wildest imaginings could she have thought that the day would turn out like it had. Just last night over dinner at the Oceanside Café, she and Linda argued about whether or not to get married in the fall. Mary Ellen was all for it. She wanted to go to town hall at midnight on the day it became legal last spring. Linda wanted to wait, however. She was out in Provincetown, and to her colleagues at the Whale Center, but most of her family didn't know she was a lesbian, or so she thought.

This was always a touchy point for Mary Ellen. In her mind she replayed the conversation they had at the restaurant last night.

"Linda, if people can't accept you for who you are, the hell with them, that's their problem!"

"Sweetie, we have been through this time and time again. My parents are old, they're not in good health and it would just be too much for them right now. They've only known I'm gay for a few years. They just wouldn't understand. Why can't we just keep things the way they are?"

"Because the way things are now, I have to pay $600 a month for my own health insurance; because the way things are now, I have no retirement plan; the way things are now, if something happened to you, I might not even be able to visit you in the hospital."

"What are you talking about, what's going to happen to me?" Linda asked.

"I'm just saying, by getting married, we can have all the same rights that straight couples have had for years. Don't you want that?"

"Of course I do, but…"

"But what?" Mary Ellen interrupted. "Are you saying you don't want those things with me? Jesus Linda, we've been together for almost five years now. If you don't want to be with me, then just go. There's thousands of women in this town, why not hook up with one of them?"

"Mary Ellen, that's not what I'm saying. I just want more time, that's all, just a little more time."

Mary Ellen recalled sliding her chair back, and standing up, looking down at her and growling, "You've had enough time to think about it Linda" and stormed out of the restaurant.

That was the last time she saw Linda alive. The realization that her final words were spoken in anger saddened her. Then the thought occurred to her that she might be considered a suspect. After all, she was already in the back seat of a police car.

The chief pulled into his space in front of the police station on Shankpainter Road. He was relieved to see that no satellite trucks had yet blocked off the parking lot. It would still take a few more hours for them to get here from Boston, but he was sure that the story was already on the wires. As he glanced up and down the street, he could see the wiry figure of Betsy Gilmore pedaling a bicycle towards him.

"We need to get inside," he said to his passengers as he

opened his door and exited. Mary Ellen momentarily panicked when she tried the handle and found it locked. Annie did the same.

"They only open from the outside, hold on." Chief Souza opened Annie's door first, then walked around the car to Mary Ellen's side. Betsy Gilmore was less than 100 yards away and closing fast.

As Mary Ellen stood up, the chief instinctively supported her by the elbow. She was nervous and her head was spinning due to the events of the past half hour.

"Let's go" said the chief.

Mary Ellen looked across the roof of the car and saw Betsy Gilmore approaching. She suddenly understood the chief's urgency to get them inside. Quickly, she made her way to the door.

The chief held the heavy glass door open as Annie and Mary Ellen made their way inside. Officer Thompson quickly buzzed them into the secure area of the building from behind the dispatch desk. Chief Souza ushered the two women into his office in the back of the building. As he closed the office door, he could hear Betsy Gilmore shrieking from the lobby.

"Chief, Chief, when's the press conference? Are those two suspects?"

"What the hell is that woman's problem?" asked Mary Ellen.

"I wish I knew," answered Chief Souza shaking his head, "but I don't want either of you to feel hounded by the press. You've been through enough today. Please, sit down."

Annie and Mary Ellen each sat in blue vinyl armchairs in front of the chief's cluttered desk. Chief Souza hung his hat on a hook on the back of the door, then sat down across from them. He glanced down at his desk and saw the remnants of what would have been his lunch, a half cup of cold coffee with a crusty ring of cream around the rim, and an enormous pile of papers that he needed to sort through. On top of all the pandemonium of Fourth of July weekend, now he had a fresh murder case on his hands.

"Okay, I'll need to take a statement from each of you. This shouldn't take very long. I'll start with you Mary Ellen. What's your full name?"

"Mary Ellen Johnson."

"Address?"

"342 Commercial Street"

"You live right on Commercial Street?"

"Yes, there's an apartment behind the gallery."

"What was your relationship to the deceased?"

"She was my partner."

"Did she live with you?"

"Yes."

"When was the last time you saw her?"

"Last night. Around 7:30. We had dinner at the Oceanside."

"You didn't see her after that?"

"No, she didn't come home."

Chief Souza paused for moment, then shifted his gaze towards Annie. "Annie, could you wait outside for a few minutes while I finish with Mary Ellen?"

Annie was flustered by all of this. "Um, okay. Mary Ellen,

she didn't come home last night? Did you two have a fight or something? Why didn't you call me?"

Mary Ellen stared down at the floor, unable to look at either of her inquisitors.

"Annie please, just wait outside. There's a waiting room down the hall to the right."

Annie quietly exited the room and closed the door. From where she stood in the hallway, she could see Betsy Gilmore sitting on a wooden bench talking on a cell phone. Fortunately, Betsy didn't see her leave the room, and Annie quickly made her way to the waiting room diagonally across the hall.

"Mary Ellen, I need you to tell me exactly what happened last night. Is Annie right? Did you two have an argument over dinner?"

"Yes, we did." Mary Ellen recalled the events of the night before to the chief.

"I just thought that she went to a friend's house for the night or something. I was pretty upset, and so was she. I just went home, cried, had a few drinks and went to bed. This morning I realized that she hadn't come home, so I tried her cell phone, then I called a few friends, then I called her office and they said she hadn't come in at all. I knew something was wrong, that wasn't like her. I walked around town this morning, looking for her in a coffee shop or somewhere, but I couldn't find her."

"Why didn't you call the police?"

This question took Mary Ellen aback. "I, I guess I thought she was just angry and wasn't talking to me." she stammered.

"How did you know to come down to MacMillan Wharf this afternoon?"

31

"Well, eventually I just went back to open up the gallery this morning around ten. It's Fourth of July weekend, so there's a lot of customers and I couldn't stay closed all day. A couple walked in talking about all the commotion down on the wharf, and how one of the whale watch boats found…her. I just knew it had to be Linda." Her voice ebbed as more tears welled in her eyes.

"Do you have any reason to think that someone would want to hurt her?"

"No, none at all. She's the nicest person I've ever met, she never did anything to anyone."

"Have you noticed any unusual people hanging around her, or the gallery? Any late night calls? Anything at all out the ordinary?"

"No. Linda's been working late a lot in the past few weeks. There have been a bunch of whales getting entangled in fishing gear, and she is on the team that responds to those, and she's been working on a big report for the government. Sometimes she's been going back to work after dinner and staying until eleven or twelve o'clock."

"What's the report about?"

"Something about how natural gas drilling on George's Bank will hurt the whales. I'm no scientist like her, but she says that it could be really bad. She was really stressed out about it. She was supposed to present the report to the EPA in Washington, D.C. in a couple of months."

"Have you seen the report?"

"No. It's mostly technical stuff anyway. Like I said, she's the scientist."

"Okay. I guess that's all for now. Do you have a number where I can reach you if anything else comes up?"

"Yeah, do you have some paper?"

The chief handed her a small notebook that he always kept in his shirt pocket and Mary Ellen wrote down her cell phone number.

"Thanks. Here's my card with my direct line and cell number. If you think of anything that might help me find who did this, give me a call anytime, day or night, okay?"

"Okay."

"Let me have an officer give you a ride home, you can go out the back door and avoid the reporters."

"Okay, I just want to go home." Mary Ellen looked deflated as she slumped in the chair. She felt lost, scared and confused, not knowing what to do next. "What should I do about funeral arrangements?"

"The county medical examiner will need to do an autopsy, they always do in a homicide. They should release the body after that. Probably Monday or Tuesday. Are you able to contact her family?"

"Yes, I have her parents' phone number." Mary Ellen grimly thought about making that call.

"I'm very sorry for your loss, Mary Ellen. I promise I'll do everything I can to catch whoever did this to Linda." He pressed a two-digit extension that rang the dispatchers desk. "Officer Thompson, I need someone to drive Ms. Johnson home. Use the back door, please."

Officer Thompson replied over the speakerphone. "OK, I'll have someone come pick her up."

The chief stood to show Mary Ellen out of the office. "Again, I'm very sorry. Thanks for you cooperation. If you'll just wait in the hall, an officer will give you a ride home in a few minutes."

"Okay," said a stunned Mary Ellen.

Annie was waiting outside the door as Mary Ellen stepped into the dimly lit hallway.

"Are you all right?" Annie asked.

"I guess so. They're giving me a ride home, but I don't want to go alone Annie. Will you come with me?"

"Sure, sure I will." She looked at the chief and he nodded in agreement.

"Annie, here's my card. Same thing I told Mary Ellen, if you can think of anything that might help us out, call me anytime."

"Okay thanks. You can always reach me at the Whale Center, or on my cell phone."

"Sure, let me write that down." The chief retrieved the notebook again from his shirt pocket. "Okay, go ahead."

While Annie told him the number, Officer Jenny O'Neal came through the back door of the station.

"Hi," Officer O'Neal said. "Where do you need to go?"

Annie told her the address of Mary Ellen's house and gallery on Commercial Street. Officer O'Neal led the two out the back door and helped them into the rear seat of her patrol car.

As Chief Souza watched them depart, he had an uneasy feeling in the pit of his stomach. He wasn't quite sure if it was sadness, hunger or a premonition of things to come. Three decades of police work had sharpened his senses and dimmed his view of humanity considerably. He didn't yet know who killed Linda Hanscomb, but he had a feeling that Mary Ellen Johnson wasn't telling him everything.

Ignoring the pile of paperwork on his desk, the Chief sat down and turned towards his computer. He opened his browser to the website of crimedata.gov, entered his password and quickly found out what Mary Ellen Johnson hadn't revealed to him.

Chapter 7

"You killed her?" Angus Black shouted down the line. Not wanting to be overheard by the secretary on the other side of the Honduran Mahogany doors, he dropped his voice down to a low, growling whisper.

He stared blankly out the window of the thirty second floor of the Harbour Towers office building in Halifax, Nova Scotia. Angus sat facing the floor-to-ceiling windows behind his desk, the early morning sun shone directly into his office. Squinting, he could see the newest of his offshore drilling rigs being built at the shipyard across the harbor in Dartmouth.

Normally, he enjoyed the view. Watching the comings and goings of the cruise ships, naval vessels and fishing boats in the morning took his mind off the many problems that faced him on a daily basis. Today, however, was different. With the telephone receiver held tightly to his ear he realized that his problems had just become exponentially greater.

"This was supposed to be a very simple operation. You go in, you find the files, make copies and leave. What in God's name happened?"

"She was there. She saw me. I was at her desk looking for the files on her computer. She must have come back for something because I watched her leave, then waited a half an hour. I was sure everyone was gone. It was late you know, almost ten o'clock. When she saw me, she just turned and ran. I knew I was busted, so I chased after her. When we got to the stairs, I caught her by the back of the hair. She started to scream, so I wrapped my arm around her neck and put my hand over her mouth. She bit me, but I held on anyway. After a while she stopped moving and I realized she was dead. I didn't mean to kill her."

Angus thought through this scenario for a moment. The

former commando was well-trained to cover his tracks and evade pursuit in hostile climates. In fact, he did so for nearly three years in Borneo during the mid 1960's while the Americans were busy losing nearby in Vietnam. After his SAS service, he returned to Scotland to study engineering at the University of Aberdeen, and then on to a PhD at Cambridge. Angus came to the U.S. in the late 70s to work at a large oil company in Houston, Texas. He had traded his military uniform for a business suit many years ago, but never forgot the lessons learned in jungle combat. First of all, leave no trace behind. "What did you do with the body?" he asked.

"I was parked outside next to the place, you know. I waited until there was nobody in the street and I put her in the back. I had a pile of nets and crap that I covered her with. I drove down to my boat and took her out to dump the body. I tied a concrete block to her feet and dropped her overboard in about 200 feet of water."

"Did anyone see you, anyone at all?"

"No, by the time I got to my boat it was after midnight. I waited until around three in the morning to head out. Nobody saw a thing."

Angus tried to regain his composure. "Do you have the files?"

"Have them? Hell no, I had to get rid of the body."

Curling the telephone tighter in his hand, Angus said "I'm not going to pay you until you get those files for me, do you understand?"

"Listen, things are going to get pretty hot around here. I've got to leave town."

"You're not going anywhere until I get those files. And if you even think of running I'll hunt you down myself. Do you understand? Now get me those damn files!" he shouted as he slammed the receiver down.

"Bloody amateur," Angus muttered. He strode across the room and opened a door concealed behind the walnut paneling of his office. He rotated the tumbler on the safe to the right, then to the left, then back to the right. As he grasped the handle and turned it, Angus could hear the muted click of the deadbolts receding into the steel housing. Glancing over to the main door of his office once more to make sure that no one could see him or the safe, he reached inside to retrieve his passport, a stack of American $100 bills, and a 9mm Glock handgun with a screw-on silencer.

After carefully packing his briefcase, with the gun concealed beneath a false bottom, he went back to his desk and picked up the phone. He dialed the two digit extension of his secretary.

A polite young woman's voice chirped, "Yes Mr. Black?"

"Karen, cancel my meetings for the rest of the day, I'm leaving early for the weekend. I'll be at my cottage up on the Mirimichi for some salmon fishing."

"Yes Mr. Black. Have a nice time, eh?"

"I'll certainly try."

"Anything else, Mr. Black?"

"No, that's all."

Angus mused that he would much rather be heading off for a quiet weekend of fly fishing than take on the tasks which he suspected he would have to complete over the next few days. It would be much quicker to tell his pilot to fly to Provincetown, but with flight plans and customs declarations, there would be far too much of a paper trail left behind. If he left now, he could cross the American border in Calais, Maine by mid-afternoon. From there, he would be in Provincetown by midnight.

Chapter 8

Annie slid into the back of the police cruiser next to Mary Ellen. This car was quite a bit older than the one in which they escaped from the crowd on MacMillan Wharf with the Chief, and as they sat down there was a noticeable creaking sound from underneath the seat. The cruiser had a sharp, stale odor that fell somewhere between locker room sweat and cat pee.

Mary Ellen was silent. She didn't look at Annie or say a word as she clambered into the car. Annie supposed that Mary Ellen was in shock. She didn't know what to say to her. Still, Annie was surprised to hear that she and Linda had an argument the night before Linda died. What had she told the chief while she was out of the room? She tried to listen through the door while she was waiting in the hall, but couldn't really make out any of their conversation.

An uncomfortable thought crept into Annie's mind. Mary Ellen couldn't have had anything to do with Linda's death, could she? Annie knew the couple only since the beginning of her internship this summer. It was only within the past month that she had spent any time with them socially.

"Sonofabitch," Mary Ellen muttered.

"What?" replied a startled Annie.

"He thinks I did it." Mary Ellen continued in a whisper so as not to be heard by Officer O'Neal.

"What are you talking about?"

"Listen, I know cops, and I know that once they get an idea into their heads, they're too stupid to try to look for the truth. They see what they want to see."

"What are you saying? Did he accuse you of something?"

"Didn't have to. His questions, his looks, the way he was talking to me. He thinks I'm hiding something, but I'm not. All I know is that Linda's dead. I don't know what to do. What should I do Annie?"

"We probably shouldn't talk about this until we get back to your place, you know." Annie's eyes shifted from Mary Ellen to the rear view mirror where she could clearly see Officer O'Neal watching them through her Oakley sunglasses.

"Right," nodded Mary Ellen.

They rode in silence the rest of the way to Mary Ellen's gallery and home on the east end of Commercial Street. As they pulled up to the front of the Dharma Gallery, Annie noticed that the door was open and that the front room was full of people.

Mary Ellen noticed this too and seemed confused that the gallery would be full of customers. She was sure she closed and locked the door hours ago when she went down to the wharf. As she approached the steps, she realized that these were not customers, but friends.

A crowd of what looked like twenty people were standing inside the front parlor of what was once a sea captain's home crying and hugging each other. Linda and Mary Ellen were well known in Provincetown amongst the local artists, innkeepers and scientists, and, in a close knit community like this one, people came together during times of tragedy and loss. Word had apparently spread quickly around town about what happened.

Annie felt conspicuous and tried to stay out of the way at the edge of the room next to a large abstract oil painting. She watched as Mary Ellen was enveloped by the crowd and disappeared from view as she and the others made their way back into the living quarters in the rear of the house. Annie was left standing alone in the gallery.

She glanced at her watch and saw that it was nearly 8:00

p.m. Peering out the window, she could see that the sky was full of violet and orange streaks from another spectacular Provincetown sunset. Knowing that Mary Ellen was surrounded by friends and supporters made her feel a little better, but Annie was also caught up with the realization that she didn't know Mary Ellen very well at all. She wanted to leave but didn't want to appear rude. She walked through the door marked "Private" into the kitchen of the old house. Mary Ellen was sitting at the table with a glass of wine. When their eyes met, Annie mouthed the words, "I'm gonna go."

Mary Ellen stood and crossed the room to give her a hug. "Thanks for being there for me, are you okay? Why don't you stay?"

"I just need to get some air. A lot's happened in the past few hours and I need to try to make some sense of it. Call me if you need anything, OK?"

"OK, Annie. Thanks."

They gave each other a quick embrace, then Annie turned and went back out through the gallery onto Commercial Street. Her cell phone rang as she walked down the steps to the sidewalk. She looked at the caller ID and was relieved that it was Shane, her boyfriend.

"Hello?"

"Hey babe, I just got in, and I'm wicked hungry. You eat yet?" asked Shane.

"I'm not hungry. Have you heard what's going on?"

"Whattya mean? Is everything OK?"

"No Shane, it's not. Linda Hanscomb's dead. She's been murdered."

Shane paused in silence at the news. Stroking his scruffy chin he said, "Damn. What happened?"

"It's a long story. Are you at the boat?"

"Yeah, I'm just hosing down the deck."

"I'm on Commercial Street now, I'll be there soon."

"Okay. Hey, you all right?"

"I don't know what I am. I just feel numb. I'll see you soon. Bye."

"Yeah, see you in few."

Annie walked down the street towards MacMillan Wharf where Shane docked his boat, the "Lady J". She hoped that the crowds were gone from where the Explorer docked. After turning the corner across from the Governor Bradford Pub, she could see the bright lights of the NEWSACTION 10 truck on the Wharf. To get to Shane's boat she would have to walk by them.

Annie walked briskly past the truck. She could see that they were still setting up for a broadcast later that night. The chief was right, she thought, Provincetown is going to be crawling with reporters pretty soon, and they'll be hounding me for comments.

She could see Shane standing at the open stern of the Lady J, hosing the last bits of herring chunks that he used to bait his lobster traps off the deck. He was wearing a set of yellow bib overalls and a white tank top, with a faded blue Red Sox cap covering his curly blond hair. Annie fell hard for him about a month after coming to Provincetown. He was tall, smart, funny and very good looking. He joked with her that it was hard to meet a straight girl in Provincetown, and as a result, he hadn't dated very much since moving back after college to take over his dad's lobster boat.

Shane's dog, Murphy, saw Annie coming and let out a series of joyful barks. Shane looked up, smiled, and turned off the hose as Annie's footsteps clanked on the welded aluminum ramp that led down to the dock.

"Hey, babe. You look awful."

"Thanks. You smell like fish."

"Missed you."

"I missed you too," she said with a kiss. This was their usual greeting.

Shane wrapped his muscular arms around Annie's tiny frame and pulled her close. She didn't care that he was wet. She didn't care that he really did smell like fish. She just needed to be held and Shane knew it.

"I'm sorry about Linda," Shane said quietly.

Annie finally let go of the tears that she had been holding back all day, and they came in a torrent.

Shane held her until she stopped sobbing. By this time it was fully dark and the moonlight twinkled on the harbor like a million diamonds. The Provincetown monument was aglow with floodlights and dance music could be heard drifting across the water from one of the many nightclubs.

"Thank you," Annie said sheepishly as she looked down at the deck, wiping her eyes on her sweatshirt sleeves. "I don't want to be alone tonight. There's just too much going on."

"I had no intention of leaving you alone. Let's go back to my house and cook up some of these bugs." Shane nodded towards a gray plastic fish tote full of lobsters resting on the gunwale of the boat.

Annie agreed and helped Shane secure the cabin of the Lady J. Each grabbed a side of the plastic tub full of live lobsters and walked up the ramp to his truck.

Chapter 9

Chief Souza pushed back his grey hair and sighed as he stared at the computer monitor. Not much surprised him anymore, and he was assured that his suspicions about Linda Hanscomb's partner were well-founded. She was indeed holding something back.

Crimedata File #00934847

RE:

Mary Ellen Johnson, a.k.a. Mary Johansson, a.k.a. Eileen Johnson, et. al.

D.O.B. 8-4-66

Height: 5'8"

Weight: 160lbs.

Hair: Brown

Ethnicity: Mixed

Current address: Unknown

Convictions:

Possession of Narcotics (Cocaine): 12-17-82, (Suspended sentence)

Possession with intent to distribute Narcotics (Cocaine): 4-03-83, (6 months served Nassau County Jail, FL)

Illegal Possession of Firearms: 7-10-85 (6 months Dade County Women's Correctional Facility, FL, 4 months served)

Solicitation: 1-23-86 (6 months suspended sentence)

<u>Murder, Second Degree</u>: 5-10-86 (10-15 years Florida State
Women's Penitentiary)

Each case had a hotlink to a case summary. Chief Souza
clicked on the blue highlighted words "Murder, Second Degree."

People vs. Johnson, Mary Ellen

5-10-86

<u>Case Summary</u>:

Mary Ellen Johnson, a.k.a Mary Johansson, a.k.a. Eileen Johnson, et.
al., was convicted of Murder in the Second Degree on the person of
Roger McNichols of Pensacola, Florida. The State of Florida
produced the case that Mr. McNichols solicited Ms. Johnson for
prostitution on 4-7-86. Mr. McNichols allegedly assaulted Ms.
Johnson, during which time Ms. Johnson discharged an unlicensed
firearm, inflicting a fatal wound to Mr. McNichols in the lower
abdomen. As a result of recent prior convictions, including Illegal
Possession of Firearms, The State of Florida sought the charge of
Murder in the Second Degree, not premeditated. This charge was
upheld by a jury of Ms. Johnson's peers. Sentence: 10-15 years at the
Florida State Women's Penitentiary.

<u>Dates of Incarceration: 5-10-86 / 8-19- 97</u>:

Ms. Johnson served her sentence without disciplinary incidents.
During this time she engaged in a correspondence course offered
through The University of Florida and obtained a Bachelor's Degree
in Fine Arts, majoring in Art History. She worked in the prison
library for 9 years as an inmate. The State of Florida approved her
parole on 8-17-97, and Ms. Johnson was released on 8-19-97 with
six months parole.

Chief Souza leaned back in his chair and locked his fingers
behind his head. Mary Ellen has kept herself out of trouble since her

release from prison, he thought. She must have made her way up to Provincetown not long afterwards. She said that she and Linda had been together for almost five years, and she had only been out of prison for about six. He wondered if this was something Mary Ellen told anyone about, or did she come here to start her life over again, as so many others had. Did Linda Hanscomb even know that her girlfriend was a drug dealer, prostitute and murderer? He felt a twinge of compassion for her, as he had seen plenty of young people get caught up in awful circumstances during his career as a cop. He set his feelings of pity aside, knowing that most murder victims know their assailants and are often involved in relationships with them. Mary Ellen sat in his office just an hour ago and admitted they had quarreled the night of the murder. He would have to keep watching her to see if she did anything foolish like try to run or cover her tracks.

It doesn't quite add up, the chief thought. The body was found over a mile offshore. Most likely it was dumped from a boat. Sure, the currents are strong off of Race Point and a body could easily get pulled out to sea from the beach in a riptide. Maybe it was an accident, or suicide.

He played out a scenario in his head where Mary Ellen and Linda Hanscomb argued. They went their separate ways, one went home, the other to the beach where she drowned herself in the waves. It wouldn't be the first time he had seen that happen here. Then, he remembered that Dr. Hanscomb's feet were tied with rope. The chief had seen his share of accidental drownings in the waters around Provincetown, but he knew there was nothing accidental about Linda Hanscomb's death.

Someone wanted her dead, and he or she didn't want the body to be found. Dr. Hanscomb spent a lot of time on the water, which always has its inherent risks. Add to that the fact that she was regularly called out to rescue ninety-foot whales weighing a hundred tons that get tangled in fishing gear. The chief surmised that she was probably someone who felt comfortable around boats.

Chief Souza knew that it would be a few hours before he could even get a preliminary report from the County Coroner pointing to a cause of death. In the meantime, he needed to retrace her final steps. Where would Linda have gone after the argument? Mary Ellen told him that Linda had been spending a lot of extra time at work for the EPA report. The chief could certainly sympathize with the idea of her having to return to the office after dinner to finish paperwork. Maybe that's where she went?

Chief Souza opened his desk drawer and pulled out a thick phone book. He looked up the number for the Whale Center, and dialed.

"Hello," a man's voice spoke.

The chief looked at his watch and was surprised to find someone answering the phone at 9:00pm, "Good evening, is this the Whale Center?"

"Yes it is. I'm Bruce Waters, director, can I help you?"

"I hope so. This is Chief Souza with the Provincetown Police."

"You're calling about Linda?"

"Yes, I am. Are you going to be there for a while? I'd like to ask some questions about Dr. Hanscomb's death, and maybe look around. Do you know if she was working there last night?"

"I don't know for sure, but there's a good chance she was. The light was on in her office when I came in this morning, and the door was left unlocked."

"Is that unusual?"

"The door being unlocked, no. People are coming and going from here all the time, especially the interns in the summer. They come in at night to check their email. But the light on in her office is out of the ordinary."

"Do you mind if come down and take a look around?"

"Not at all. Anything I can do to help."

"I'm leaving now. I should be there in about ten minutes."

"Okay. I'll meet you downstairs. Goodbye.

"Thanks. Goodbye."

As the chief hung up the phone, he noticed the red message light was blinking. He dialed his voice mailbox number and retrieved six messages, all from various reporters asking when there would be a press conference. He deleted them all. On his way out, he said "Carla, tell the reporters that I'll be holding a press conference here at nine o'clock tomorrow morning."

He strode out of the station and slid behind the wheel of his Crown Victoria. Looking at the clock, he realized that he had been at work for fourteen hours. "Damn." he muttered under his breath.

Ten minutes later, Chief Souza parked his car in the street next to the Whale Center. It looked like most of the other old, white clapboard houses in the West End of Provincetown, except for a large hand-carved sign depicting a right whale over the front door. He approached the steps and saw someone coming through the door to meet him.

"Hi, I'm Chief Souza. Are you Bruce Waters?"

"Yes." he said glumly as he extended his hand.

Chief Souza took it and shook twice. "Thanks for letting me come over on such short notice."

"Sure, anything I can do to help find out what happened to Linda. She meant the world to me. I don't know what we're going to do without her around here."

"It sounds like you two were close."

"Close. Yeah, you could say that. Linda was my wife."

Chief Souza repressed a nearly uncontrollable urge to scratch his head. Instead he just stood in the doorway with an incredulous look on his face. "But," he stammered, "I thought she was, um, you know, gay."

"She is, only she didn't know that when we got married. Come on in."

The chief accepted the invitation. *If this was the last place Linda was before she was killed, I might be able to find some evidence here,* he thought.

Bruce started talking as he led Chief Souza inside. "We met in graduate school. We were working on our Ph.D.'s at the time, and we both shared a love of the ocean. When the director's position opened up here, I jumped at the chance to have it. We got married just before we moved here, but that was twelve years ago. After working here for a few years, Linda started to have more feelings for women than for me. I guess she felt like she could really be herself here."

"How'd that make you feel?"

"Well, I wasn't too happy about it. At first I was furious. I wanted her out of the house and out of my life. But after I cooled down a bit I realized that I still cared about her a lot, and her work was invaluable to the center. I agreed to a divorce, and we were both able to move on with our lives. Until now, that is. I don't know what I'm going to do without her. We worked as a team to run this place."

Standing inside the foyer of the old house, Chief Souza could see that this was a busy office. Desks were covered in paperwork, marine charts hung on the walls with colored push pins marking recent whale sightings, and a fax machine sat in the corner with a pile of new arrivals in the tray. It reminded him of his office down the street. Still, it was nearly 9:30 at night, late even by workaholic standards.

"Do you usually work this late?" the chief queried.

"During the summer, yeah. We're operating ten whale watch trips a day on two boats; monitoring Coast Guard, fisheries, and shipping radio channels for whale sightings; and we're always ready to respond to a whale entanglement or marine mammal stranding. Things slow down a bit in the winter. The volunteers and interns are gone, and it was pretty much Linda, me, and two other staff members running the place."

Chief Souza sympathized with Bruce. He suspected that rather than deal with Linda's death and allow himself to grieve, he was busying himself with work. He had done the same thing after his own wife died.

"Did you see Linda here last night?"

"Yeah. It was around 8:30 or so. She often came in at night to work on reports and grants. I was just leaving for the night, so I asked her to lock up."

"Did she look upset at all?"

"No, not really. Not anything that I noticed. She just came in and went upstairs to her office."

"Hmmm. OK." Chief Souza was having doubts about Mary Ellen's story. "Could you show me where that is?"

"Sure, it's this way."

Bruce led the chief up the creaky wooden staircase to the second floor. A long central hallway ran the length of the building with doors on either side. At the top of the stairs was a door with a small sign on it that read:

Linda Hanscomb, Ph.D., Associate Director.

"This is her office," Bruce said as he flipped on the overhead lights.

Chief Souza looked around, then asked, "Does this door lock?"

"No, the only locks are on the front and back doors, and the barn where we keep the Zodiacs."

"Has anyone been in here today?"

"I don't know. They told me she didn't come in at all today. But I doubt anyone would come in here without her."

"Where were you today?"

"I was out on a whale watch boat all day. I didn't get back here until almost seven."

The chief scanned the office for any clues. He noticed that while all the books were neatly arranged on the shelves, there were loose papers strewn about on the floor behind the desk. He bent over to look at some of them. "Could you tell me what these are?"

Bruce squatted and picked up some of the papers. "Research, data on phytoplankton blooms on George's Bank, whale sightings. What is this stuff doing all over the floor? This isn't like her."

"What do you mean?"

"She's a neat freak. Linda always had everything in order. That's why we worked so well together. I was the one with the big ideas, but she was the one who kept everything running smoothly." Bruce bit his lower lip and thought for a moment. "You know, I think someone has been in here."

That was also Chief Souza's impression. "Mr. Waters, I'm going to call the State Police Crime Lab. They're going to comb this building looking for clues. I think this might have been where Linda was killed. I'm afraid that we can't let anyone else in here until they've finished."

Bruce needed a moment to take in the Chief's use of the word "killed." "Here? Oh. Wow. Okay. How long do you think that will take?"

"Can't say. They probably won't get here until morning."

"I just can't believe this is happening. Yesterday she was here, today…" Bruce's voice trailed off and the chief could see tears welling in his eyes. "Why did this happen to her? I don't understand. She never hurt anyone."

"I'm very sorry, Mr. Waters. I'm going to do everything I can to figure out what happened to Linda and bring whoever did this to justice. I promise."

"Yeah. Okay. Um, what should I do?"

"Just go home and get some rest. Will you be available tomorrow if I need to reach you?"

"I'm always available. I live across the street. Just come over if you need anything. I'll be around all day."

"Okay, thanks. Do you mind if I stay here and look around for a while?"

"Sure. Just lock the door when you leave, OK?" Bruce said quietly as he left Linda's office.

Chief Souza heard Bruce walk down the stairs and, moments later, the wooden screen door slam as he left. Finally, he had a chance to look around. From what Bruce had told him, Linda Hanscomb was meticulous in her work and wouldn't leave a pile of papers on the floor. They were tossed in a hurry, probably by her killer, while looking for something specific. But what?

He stepped outside the office into the hallway. Looking around for any sign of a struggle, his eyes were drawn to a small shadow cast on the wall next to the stair landing. He kneeled down closer to get a better view. The plaster was cracked in a round depression about the size of an orange. He shined his flashlight on the damaged spot and could clearly see three strands of light blond hair stuck to the impression.

Chief Souza unclipped the radio from his belt and activated the microphone.

"Dispatch? This is Chief Souza. Over."

"Hi, Chief, it's Carla. Over."

"Carla, I'm at the Whale Center in the West End. I need a team down here with evidence kits as soon as possible. Call the State Police Crime Lab, too. We're going to need them in the morning. Over."

"Okay Chief, just a moment." The radio went silent for ten seconds while Officer Thompson switched channels. "I have officers on their way. Over."

"Thanks Carla. Any word on the Hanscomb autopsy? Over."

"Not yet, Chief. Over."

"Okay, thanks. Out."

Chief Souza waited in silence in the empty building, mentally trying to construct a scenario of what happened the night before. He envisioned Linda Hanscomb struggling in her office with an intruder, being thrown down the stairs, smacking her head hard into the wall. That probably wouldn't be enough to kill her, he thought, but maybe knock her unconscious.

He could see blue flashing lights outside the windows as his backup arrived. The Chief descended the stairs and stepped out the front door where he looked toward the house across the street. Glancing up, he noticed a light on in an upstairs room. He could clearly see Bruce making a phone call and having what looked like an animated discussion. Chief Souza watched as Bruce slammed the phone down onto its receiver, turned and stared out the window. For just an instant, Bruce Waters and Chief Souza's eyes met. Bruce backed quickly away from the window and pulled down the shade. Moments later, the lights in the room went out.

Chief Souza pulled his notebook and a pen out of his shirt pocket and began to write a to-do list including fingerprint analysis and a full background check on Bruce Waters.

Just then his cell phone rang. He walked over to his car and leaned on the roof as he answered. "Hello, this is Chief Souza."

Chapter 10

With both hands, Shane grabbed the gray plastic fish tub that Annie had been helping him carry. In one swift move, he heaved it up into the bed of his truck and slid nearly sixty pounds of lobsters into the back. Annie was impressed by how such a physically strong man could also be so tender and gentle. These qualities are what originally caught her attention as she spotted him at the Governor Bradford in June, where he was watching a Red Sox game at the bar. They chatted about the game and, when it was over, they strolled to the end of MacMillan Wharf to look at the stars. They talked about science, nature, Provincetown, and the ocean. There, they shared their first kiss. That's where she fell for with Shane, and his decrepit 1978 Ford pickup truck.

The tailgate had rusted off and been discarded years ago. The bed of the truck was full of the detritus of a commercial fisherman, empty fish totes, orange and green netting, empty five gallon buckets, and the remains of various sea creatures who had their first and last glimpses of terrestrial life at Shane's hands. Shane joked that the truck was older than he was, and that was no exaggeration. His father had bought the truck from another fisherman in the early 1980's and drove it everyday thereafter. Shane learned to drive behind the wheel of this truck, learned how to kiss a girl in the front seat at the Wellfleet Drive-In, and learned how to make love in the back of the truck one night under the stars at Cahoon's Hollow.

When his father died suddenly of a heart attack last year, Shane decided to continue the family fishing business until all of his father's legal and financial affairs were resolved. After a few weeks, he fell in love with the freedom, the excitement, and the sense of peace that he found out on the water.

Shane had always worked during the summers alongside his father on the Lady J, but had never taken her out alone until three days after his father's funeral when he realized that the lobster pots hadn't been checked in over a week. He couldn't leave $100,000 worth of gear out in the water unattended. His father managed 200 lobster traps around Cape Cod Bay by himself. Shane figured that since he was not even half his father's age, he should be able to do the same, and he did. It didn't take him long to realize that he had a profitable business that he enjoyed, in one of the most beautiful places on earth. Shane knew quickly that he would follow in his father's and grandfather's footsteps and make a living at sea.

Annie climbed into the cab of the truck and slid across the tattered vinyl seat so that she could be closer to Shane. Murphy jumped in the back, assigning himself the duty of lobster guardian. He sniffed wildly around the lobsters and the tangle of nets.

Shane turned the ignition key, and the old beast fired up with a snort. Turning on the headlights, Shane could see the television news staff milling about on the wharf, waiting for their late night broadcast.

"Oh man" he sighed, "are they here about Linda?"

"Yeah, the police chief said the town would be full of reporters by morning. They'll be coming from all over."

"Any of them try to talk to you?"

"No, well sort of, but I didn't say anything."

"That's good, Annie. Don't talk to them, they'll just take everything you say and twist it around, or make you look like a fool."

"Mmmm. I really don't want to talk them. I just want to erase today from my mind, like it never happened, you know?" Annie paused for a few moments, then said, "I found her. Did you know that?"

"No, I didn't." Shane turned pale and jittery at her

announcement. "Jesus, Annie, what happened?"

Annie recounted the story of the screaming tourists, and how she and Juicy pulled Linda's body on board. "Juicy said that I fainted when I saw her. I can't believe it, but when I came to, he was right there with me."

"Juicy's a good guy. He's been coming up here every summer from Jamaica for years. I'm glad he was there. I'm just sorry I wasn't."

"Don't be. There's nothing you could have done. I'm just freaked out that somebody would murder Linda. What for? She was so nice. Everybody liked her."

Shane paused for a few moments before saying "Not everybody."

Annie shot him a glare. "That's really mean, Shane."

"I don't mean it like that, what I mean is that the Whale Center has done a lot of good research, but it's cost fishermen some serious money. I support most of what they've done, but I have to use a sinking rope now on the lobster traps that costs four times what the nylon rope does. That cost me thousands of dollars last year alone. Linda was the author of that report and it became law based on her recommendations."

"Do you know how many whales get entangled each year in lobster trap lines Shane? Dozens. I've been out on some rescues this summer with Linda. It's terrible to see. The ropes get tangled around their mouths and cut into their flesh. Sometimes it makes it so they can't feed and they starve to death over a period of months or they die of infections. The sinking ropes keep the lines on the sea floor so that the whales don't get entangled. Don't you think that's worthwhile?"

"It's not that it's a bad idea, Annie. It's a good idea. I don't want to hurt whales or lose my gear because of entanglement. But each of these new regulations makes it harder to earn a living as a fisherman. Every year it's something. New gear, reduced number of days at sea, shorter fishing seasons, lower quotas, it's always something. Conservation is fine, Annie, but these rules are wiping out an entire way of life. A lot of people have gone out of business in the last decade and lost everything. The banks foreclose on their houses, their boats are scrapped, it's just awful. So, the little guys who have a marginal impact on fish stocks are driven out of business and the only ones who can survive are the giant trawlers that stay out at sea for months at a time, wiping out what's left. It just doesn't make sense."

They rode in silence for a few minutes, with the exception of Murphy sniffing around the lobsters and occasionally barking through the sliding window in the cab of the truck. Annie was thinking about her prior arguments with Shane on these issues when a new idea dawned on her. "Wait a minute. Are you saying you think a fisherman killed Linda?"

Shane bit his lower lip and exhaled slowly. "I wouldn't bet against it. I know guys who see the whole conservation movement as a threat to their existence and their way of life. When people feel backed into a corner, they're likely to fight."

"Do you see it that way?"

"No. I think we all want the same things, plenty of fish in the ocean, clean water, a healthy economy, and a nice community to raise our kids."

"Our kids?" Annie said coyly.

He put his hand around Annie's shoulder and squeezed her in tightly towards him. Teasingly he said, "Sure, someday, when I meet the right girl." Annie felt safe with his muscular arm around her. She leaned her head onto Shane's shoulder and said nothing more as they drove to his house.

Ten minutes later, the creaking old truck crunched onto the

crushed-shell driveway of Shane's house in North Truro. Neither he nor his father were very particular about the décor of the home, but it had a magnificent view over Cape Cod Bay and Provincetown. The house was built by Shane's grandfather just after World War II and was where both Shane and his father had been raised.

Shane hoisted the lobsters out of the back of the truck and brought them into the garage where he kept a tank full of re-circulating salt water. This way, he could keep the lobsters fresh and alive until the market price increased. This was the equivalent of an investor timing the stock market which when done well could increase his profits substantially.

"Do you need some help?" Annie asked.

"No thanks. I've got 'em. Here, take these." Shane handed her three large, wriggling lobsters for dinner. She was used to this, as they ate lobster at least two nights a week. The first time she had dinner with Shane she was surprised to see him put two lobsters in the pot for each of them. Annie enjoyed the sweet richness of the lobster, but was full after one. By the time Shane had nearly finished his second crustacean, she told him that she was too full to eat another. He said "No problem" and placed Annie's unfinished lobster on his plate. She had never seen a man eat like this before and was a little repulsed at his savagery. After a few days however, Annie came to realize that working a vigorous ten to twelve hour day at sea, by himself, Shane worked up a sizeable appetite.

Their dinner routine had become established by now. Shane would take a long, hot shower, as Annie insisted he do, while she put a pot of boiling water on the stove to cook the lobsters. She searched through the refrigerator to find some kind of vegetable or salad greens to accompany the "bugs". By the time she had made the side dishes, the water was boiling. Annie waited for Shane to get out of the shower to do the dirty work. As much as she enjoyed their lobster feasts, she still couldn't bring herself to dispatch the lobsters into the boiling water.

Shane emerged from the shower clean shaven and having lost most of the odor of fish that he acquired through the day. In what seemed like one swift motion, he pulled the lid off the pot, dropped the unfortunate lobsters in, replaced the lid, opened the refrigerator and pulled the tops off of two Budweisers. Handing one to Annie, he said, "Cheers".

"Thanks," Annie replied always impressed by Shane's smoothness. Clinking his bottle with hers, she said, "I made a salad. Do you want to eat on the porch?"

"Sure." The two stepped outside onto the screened-in porch, sat down in the double Adirondack chair that Shane made with his dad, and stared out to sea.

Shane finally broke the silence. "It's a nice night isn't it?" When Annie didn't reply, he looked over at her and said, "What's wrong?"

"It's not a nice night, Shane. In fact, it's a lousy night. In fact, it sucks. There's a murderer out there somewhere walking around while Linda's lying in the morgue, and you're acting like there's nothing wrong!" Annie paused for a moment, realizing that she'd snapped at him. It was too late to retract her words. "What you said before, do you really think a fisherman did it?"

"I'm sorry Annie, I just don't know what to feel right now. I know you really looked up to her and all. As far as who killed her, I've no idea. I mean, it could be a local guy. It had to be someone with a boat right?"

"Yeah. Do you know anybody who would do it? Anyone who hated her that much?"

"A lot of the guys talk trash. And everybody hates the regulations. Maybe somebody got drunk and went crazy, but I haven't heard anything about it. How's Mary Ellen doing?"

"She's in bad shape. It's such a huge loss for her and she

thinks the police chief is trying to blame her for the murder."

"What do you mean? How?."

"I guess she and Linda had a big fight or something last night when they were out for dinner. I don't know a lot of other details, though; that's when the chief asked me to leave so he could question Mary Ellen alone."

"He was questioning her?"

"I guess that's what you'd call it. Anyway, she seemed really upset. At least she had a bunch of friends at her place to take care of her. That's where I was coming from when you called."

"Is it possible?"

"Is what possible?"

"That she did it. Do you think Mary Ellen might have killed Linda?"

This was exactly the question that Annie was asking herself, but she didn't want to admit it. "I don't know. I don't really know her all that well. I've worked with Linda for a few months, and been out with her and Mary Ellen a few times. She seems O.K., but she does get kind of excited easily."

"What do you mean excited?"

"It's weird. She gets really defensive about things. You can't really joke with her, or she takes it the wrong way. Linda said that Mary Ellen had been through a lot of hard times and she was touchy about it, but I've seen her get a look in her eye when she's mad that's kind of scary. Maybe she did it. Oh, my God! Do you think she killed her?"

"Anything's possible, Annie. I'd stay away from her if I were you. You don't want to get pulled into this any more than you already are."

Just then the kitchen timer dinged, signaling that the lobsters were ready.

"I'll get 'em," Shane said.

"I'm not hungry anymore."

"Oh come on, you've got to eat."

Shane stood and went inside to pluck the lobsters from the pot and melt some butter in the microwave. Annie searched in her pocket for Chief Souza's business card. "Should I call him?" she whispered to herself. Pulling the cell phone out of the other pocket of her tan shorts, she punched in the chief's cell phone number.

"Hello, this is Chief Souza."

"Chief, it's Annie Macalister. I'm sorry for calling so late. Are you busy?" She knew she sounded nervous.

"Busy trying to find a killer. Where are you, Annie?"

"I'm at my boyfriend's place in Truro. Why?"

"I just want to make sure you're safe."

Annie gulped. "Do you have a reason to think I'm not?"

Chief Souza could hear the tension rising in her voice. "It's possible that whoever killed Dr. Hanscomb was after her research. It looked like her office was ransacked. I suggest you lay low for a couple of days. Stay away from the Whale Center. What did you say your boyfriend's name was?"

"I didn't say. But it's Shane Costa. Why?"

"I know Shane. Nice kid. Too bad about his father. He took over the boat, right?"

"Yeah. Um, Chief, the reason I called was that I'm worried about Mary Ellen."

"How so?"

"I don't know exactly, but maybe you could swing by and check on her. She gets very emotional, and she seemed really upset when we left the police station today."

"How well do you know her?"

"I was just telling Shane, not very well at all."

"Annie, this is off the record. I would keep my distance from Mary Ellen Johnson if I were you. I'm concerned about her as well, and I'll keep my eyes open for anything unusual. Is there anything else?"

"No, I guess that's it. Do you really think somebody might come after me?"

"I don't mean to alarm you, but we really don't know what we're dealing with here. Just keep a low profile for a few days and keep your cell phone on at all times. I'll stay in touch with you. Don't worry, it's probably nothing, but I would rather be safe than sorry."

"Me too. What about work?"

"I'll make sure Billy looks out for you. You'll be safe on the boat with him."

"OK, I guess. Thanks. Bye."

"Goodbye."

Shane stepped out onto the porch with a stainless steel bowl full of steaming red lobsters and two plates. "Who was that?"

"Chief Souza."

Shane's jaw dropped. "Why did he call?"

"He didn't. I called him. I'm worried about Mary Ellen, what's wrong with that?"

Shane stared at her for a moment. "You just need to worry about yourself. What'd he say?"

"He told me to stay here with you and only come into town for work."

Shane looked surprised. "Really? He said that?"

"Yeah. He said Billy would watch out for me on the boat."

"Wait a minute. He thinks someone's after you?"

"He doesn't know, but just in case."

"Just in case what?"

"I don't know Shane. What should I do?"

He sat down next to her and wrapped his arm around her slender shoulders. He leaned in and whispered in her ear. "Stay with me."

"I will," Annie replied placing a delicate kiss on his lips.

"No, I mean come out on the boat with me tomorrow. I need to go check the pots off of Dennis. I'll be out there all day. Nobody would know where you are, you'd be totally safe."

"What about work?"

"Call Billy. Tell him that you need a day off. After the day you've had, I don't think anyone would expect you to come to work tomorrow. You need a day off. Here dig in." Shane dropped a lobster on a plate and handed it to Annie.

"I'm really not hungry. I'll just eat the salad."

"Suit yourself."

She watched with a mixture of awe and disgust as Shane twisted the tails off three lobsters, extracted the meat with a dinner fork, and dropped it into a bowl of melted butter. He ate like a Neanderthal, but despite this, she knew she was smitten. Shane finished off the three lobsters in under ten minutes and washed them down with his beer. One loud belch later, he sat back in the Adirondack chair with a satisfied look on his face. "Those were good. You sure you don't want anything else?"

"I'm sure, yeah. Thanks. I think I'll get ready for bed, actually. I'm really wiped out."

"After the day you've had, I can understand. I'll clean up."

"Thanks." Annie kissed him again as she stood up. She could still taste the butter on his lips.

Moments later, Shane could hear the shower running. He looked forward to joining Annie in bed. It had been nearly a week since she spent the night. However, in the time it took to wash the dishes, brush his teeth, and turn out the lights, she was sound asleep.

He undressed and laid down on the bed next to her. Lightly, he traced his fingertips along the outline of her breast through the one clean t-shirt that she had found in his dresser. Shane hoped that she would wake and be interested in making love, but Annie rolled onto her side away from him. He was disappointed, but not surprised. After all, it had been a horrible day.

Chapter 11

"Is your trip for business or pleasure?" The US Customs agent asked.

"Business," replied Angus Black.

"What sort of business are you in?"

"Real estate."

"Uh-huh. Where are you going?"

"I have a meeting in Boston tomorrow afternoon."

"So, you're staying in Boston?"

"I'll probably stay in Bangor tonight, then drive down in the morning."

"That's a good idea. It's about four hours to Boston from here and it's pretty late."

Glancing at the analog clock on the dashboard of his Lexus, Angus realized that it was after eleven already. "Yes, it is."

"Are you transporting any alcohol, cigarettes, or firearms?"

"No." Angus lied on all three counts. He hoped he wouldn't be subject to a search. In his experience, crossing the U.S. border as a clearly affluent, white male in his sixties rarely raised an eyebrow. This time was no different.

"OK, then, enjoy your trip. Watch out for moose between here and Bangor."

"I'll do that, thank you. Have a nice night."

"You too, sir. Next!" The agent handed Angus back his passport and waived the car behind him forward.

Angus drove over the St. Croix River bridge separating St. Stephen, New Brunswick from Calais, Maine. The two towns seemed remarkably similar at night and the distinction between the two countries appeared to be quite arbitrary. The streets of Calais were nearly deserted, except for a short line of cars and tractor trailers waiting to be processed through Canadian Customs. He would spend the night in Bangor, and make his way to Provincetown the next day. Now that he had passed through the border, there was nothing but 350 miles of highway between him and his target.

Angus had formulated his plan during the drive from Halifax to the border. He would drive to Boston and leave his car in a commuter garage. From there he would walk to Rowe's Wharf where he would then board the fast ferry to Provincetown. All of this could be paid for in cash and allow him a sense of anonymity by moving in a crowd. He would be dressed casually, as a tourist might, and carry a small bag that contained a single change of clothes, a large sum of American dollars, and his gun.

He planned to call his accomplice and arrange a meeting for payment. Being a man of his word, he would first show him the cash, then execute him if need be. Timed correctly, he would return on the ferry to Boston the next morning and be back in Halifax late that night. Problem solved, he hoped.

It had been many years since The Bull undertook a mission like this one. Angus felt a calm excitement that he had not known since his paratrooper days over three decades ago. His experiences in Southeast Asia had taught him that overconfidence could lead to sloppiness and defeat, and he could afford neither. This had to be quick, clean, and well-timed. He could leave no trace behind and he would take every step to ensure that. Angus hoped that by the time anyone noticed that his accomplice was missing, he would be back in Canada.

The sixty mile, two-lane stretch of Route 9 between Calais and Bangor, Maine is lonely and dark. There are only a few small hamlets in between, with much of the land part of unincorporated townships. Angus had driven this road a few times before, but never so late at night. Once he left the glow of Calais' fast food restaurants and gas stations, he was in near complete darkness, save for the road illuminated by his Xenon headlights. Angus felt like he was driving through a tunnel.

He glanced down to change the CD in the car's audio system. He clicked through the six discs which he had loaded to keep him awake on this dark stretch of road. Angus settled on the Rolling Stones greatest hits. The opening tribal drumbeats of "Sympathy for the Devil" erupted through the ten speakers in the cabin of the Lexus.

Angus looked up just in time to see a black wall of fur less than one hundred feet away in his headlights. He stomped on the brake pedal and felt the thumping of his anti-lock brakes kicking into action as the moose stared incredulously at him. The moose took two steps forward and Angus narrowly missed it.

Shaken, he sat in the driver's seat, feeling that this might be a forewarning of things to come. "Pay attention, Angus" he said aloud.

After an hour, Angus reached Bangor and spotted a small, nondescript motel alongside the highway with a neon vacancy sign illuminated. He parked in front of the lobby. When he entered, he found a young woman of Indian or Pakistani origin watching MTV on a black and white television behind the counter.

"Can I help you?" she said in her lilting accent.

"Do you have any rooms available?"

"Yes, sir. For how many?"

"Just me."

"Smoking or non?"

"Smoking please."

"I have a queen bed, smoking, for $49.95."

"Fine." Angus said pulling a crisp $100 bill from his wallet.

"Your name, please?"

"Thomas E. Lawrence." He enjoyed using this pseudonym when he traveled. He had yet to come across a hotel clerk who recognized the name of the man better known as Lawrence of Arabia.

"OK, Mr. Lawrence, here is your change, and your key, Room 17. Checkout is at ten o'clock. We have coffee and tea starting at seven."

"Thanks," Angus mumbled as he took the key and his change off of the peeling Formica counter.

"Have a good night."

"You, too."

Angus glanced across the parking lot and saw where his room was located. He moved his car so that it was obscured from the road by a large SUV. He entered the room and found it to be stifling hot. After relieving himself in the bathroom, he opened the windows and turned on the air conditioning in an attempt to cool the room. There was no chair, so he sat on the bed. Turning on the television, he clicked through the channels until he found some soft-core pornography on HBO. He closed the windows and turned the air conditioner to high. He laid down on the bed fully clothed, and in his exhausted state, drifted off to a restless sleep.

Chapter 12

Annie slept fitfully that night. Her dreams were a constant loop of her and Juicy pulling Linda's bloated body onto the deck of the Explorer. Sometimes the dreams would wake her and she would be momentarily disoriented until she felt Shane lying next to her.

One version of the dream was very detailed. She saw Linda upstairs at the Whale Center, struggling with a large man who was choking her. This dream in particular stood out, as she could sense the stale smell of sweat and alcohol from Linda's killer. It was as if she were standing there, helplessly watching it all happen. In her sleep she cried out, "No! no!," then she sat bolt upright in bed, covered in sweat and out of breath.

"It's OK, Annie, it's just a dream," said a startled Shane trying to soothe her.

"My god Shane, it was like I was there. I could see Linda being strangled by some guy."

"What did he look like?"

"I don't know. He was looking right at me and he stank like booze and body odor."

"You could smell him in your dream?" he asked quizzically.

"Yeah. Sometimes I have really detailed dreams."

"Try to get some sleep, Annie. We're leaving early in the morning."

"OK."

She never considered herself to be clairvoyant or psychic, but from time to time, Annie had a dream that was so clear that she remembered every detail. The first time she remembered having a dream like this was the night her grandmother died. Annie was twelve years old that summer. In her dream she was in her grandmother's kitchen, watching her bake one of her famous apple pies. The dream seemed so real that Annie could smell the cinnamon and apples baking.

When her grandmother took the pie out of the oven, she turned to Annie and said, "I'm your angel now, Annabel. I'll always be watching out for you." She set the pie down on the table in front of her, and disappeared.

The next morning Annie awoke to the phone ringing, followed by her mother crying. When she went downstairs to see what was wrong, her mom hugged her close and through her tears said "Grandma died last night, sweetheart. Uncle Jimmy said that she just passed away in her sleep. He found her on the couch this morning when he went over to mow the lawn."

Ever since then, Annie's memory of her grandmother was a source of comfort and reassurance. She pictured her grandmother's face in her mind as she drifted back to sleep.

Annie awoke feeling a warm, strong body snuggled up against her. She always enjoyed waking up with Shane. Annie rolled over to return the caress and was greeted with a cold wet nose and a slobbering kiss from Murphy, Shane's boisterous, loveable, black Labrador.

She wiped her face and laughed. Murphy was lying on the bed next to her, tail thumping on the mattress like a bass drum. "Hi Murphy" she groaned. The attention only made his tail thump harder as he playfully chewed on her hand, covering her with drool.

"Ick! Yuck! Shane! Get him off me! Shane!" she called out in a mixture of laughter and revulsion.

"Come on Murph! Let's eat!" Shane called from the kitchen. These words were as magical to Murphy as they were to Shane. The big dog quickly rolled over, stood up on the mattress, shook himself, jumped down to the floor, and trotted into the kitchen. Annie breathed a sigh of relief.

With the window shades up she could see that it was just before dawn and the orange sunlight danced on the waters of Cape Cod Bay. She glanced at the alarm clock on the nightstand next to her, which read 5:15. Shane liked to get an early start to be out on the water during the calm of the morning. She couldn't blame him. Annie had learned from being on the whale watch boats all summer that Cape Cod Bay can be as smooth as glass in the morning and be churning with whitecaps by late afternoon.

"You want eggs?" Shane hollered from the kitchen.

"OK. I'm gonna shower first."

"You just showered last night," Shane said quizzically.

"Yeah, well, your dog slobbered all over me."

"Sorry 'bout that. He's just saying good morning. Bacon?"

"Sure. I'll be out in a few minutes."

Annie pulled back the quilt and stood up wearing panties and a T-shirt. The cool morning air made her shiver as she stepped quickly into the bathroom. She turned the shower on to warm up while she conducted her morning routine. Yesterday seemed like a bad dream to her and very far away. As the tiny bathroom filled with steam, Annie's head started to fill with questions.

She knew that she wouldn't go in to work today, but what about tomorrow? There were still a few more weeks of summer and she needed the money. What about Linda's research? She could finish it. She'd been helping her compile data most mornings that she wasn't guiding a whale watch. She knew what had to be done. She would have to call Bruce Waters anyway to let him know that she wasn't coming in.

As she stepped into the warm shower, Annie thought about Linda. Would there be a funeral? What would Mary Ellen do now? And why did the Chief urge her to stay away from her? He must know a lot more than he's letting on. Mary Ellen said that the chief was suspicious of her; maybe he had a good reason. So many questions and she had so few answers. Annie hated the uncertainty. She hoped that the warm water running over her would wash away her concerns, but it didn't. She replayed the dream in her head over and over, trying to remember the physical details of Linda's killer. As hard as she tried, all she could remember was the smell and Linda's muffled scream.

After she showered and dried her hair with a towel, she put on a clean pair of bikini briefs, her bra from the day before, and a pair of shorts. She went through Shane's pile of laundry and found a white Land's End Marine T-shirt to wear.

"There you are. Feel better?" Shane asked as she entered the kitchen.

"Yeah, thanks. Mmmm, that smells good." The cozy smell of bacon filled the house. Seeing a heap of it on a plate, Annie gasped. "Good Lord Shane, how much did you make?"

"Just one package. Why?"

"A whole pound of bacon?"

"It's good. Have some. If there's any left over we can make BLT's for lunch." He tossed a small piece of bacon to Murphy who snapped it out of the air and licked his chops.

Annie put a small scoop of scrambled egg on her plate with two pieces of bacon. She opened the refrigerator and helped herself to a glass of orange juice. Sitting down at the little wooden table in the kitchen, she said "Do you think I'm in danger?"

Shane barely glanced up from his plate to answer, "From what?"

"From whoever killed Linda."

"Why would anyone want to hurt you?"

"That's what Linda probably thought."

"The chief scared you last night didn't he?"

"Yeah, he did."

"Look, I think they'll find who did this pretty quick. Linda Hanscomb was well-known around P-town. Someone's gonna talk. I don't think you have anything to worry about. Want some coffee?"

"Not yet, thanks."

"Anyway, nobody even knows why she was killed. It probably had nothing to do with her work. It could have been a robbery, or anything."

"I guess so." Annie sounded less than convinced.

"So, you want to come with me today, right?"

"Yeah. When do we need to leave?"

"Whenever you're ready. I just need to brush my teeth."

"Okay. I'll clean up."

"Thanks." Shane leaned in to kiss the top of Annie's head, then marched off towards the bathroom. Murphy lifted himself off the floor and followed, tail wagging the whole way.

Annie put the breakfast dishes and pans in the dishwasher, then found some plastic ware for the bacon. Shane had eaten at least half of it, so there wasn't much hope of making sandwiches for later. Instead, she took a loaf of bread and made a small stack of peanut butter and jelly sandwiches. With lunch packed and both ready to go, they climbed into the old truck with Murphy drooling in between them on the bench seat.

Annie looked forward to spending the day with Shane. The sun was rising over the dunes and Pilgrim Lake on their way into Provincetown, causing an orange glare that necessitated both of them to put on sunglasses, even at 6:00 in the morning. As they rolled into town, the streets were quiet. There was no hint of the pandemonium of the preceding night. Each bed and breakfast had a little sign saying "full" or "No Vacancy," which was the only indication of just how packed the little town was for the holiday weekend.

The old pickup creaked down MacMillan Wharf, and Annie could see five large, white vans, each with a big number on the side and the call letters of the television station they serviced. The chief was right, Annie thought, this was a big story. She was glad that she would be spending the day baiting lobster traps with Shane instead of ducking reporters.

As they passed the Explorer's dock, Annie saw Billy Souza in the ticket booth, preparing for the day. "Stop the truck, Shane, I need to talk to Billy for a second."

"OK"

The trucked slowed to a squeaky halt next to the ticket booth on MacMillan Wharf. Hearing this, Billy stepped out of the tiny booth to see who it was. When he realized it was Annie, a big, compassionate smile appeared on his usually stoic face.

"Annie, what are you doing up this early? How ya' feeling?"

"I'm OK, thanks. Will you be all right without me today? I really need some time to recover from yesterday."

"Of course Annie. Don't worry about it. Take the day. You're on again Monday right?"

"Yeah, I think so."

"OK, then, have a good weekend. You can make up the hours next week. You and Shane heading out?"

"Yeah. We're going lobstering."

"Looks like a good day for it. Take it easy, Annie. Good seeing you, Shane."

"You too," Shane replied.

In a lowered voice Annie said, "Thanks for your help yesterday, Billy."

He placed his hand on her arm and said, "Don't worry about it. Just go enjoy yourself. You deserve it."

"Thanks."

"Have a good one." Billy gently squeezed her arm. Had Shane not been sitting in the truck he would have tried to give her a hug.

Annie looked into his eyes and noticed an affection that she hadn't seen before. She felt a small stirring in her belly as she climbed back into the truck. "Thanks, Billy, see you Monday."

The transmission clunked into drive as Shane took his foot off the brake and he drove the last hundred feet to the end of the wharf. He parked in front of the Lady J. As soon as Shane opened his door, Murphy bounded out and ran down the ramp towards the boat, chasing away three herring gulls. As Annie stepped out of the truck, she could hear someone swearing loudly from inside one of the docked fishing boats.

"Goddamn it! Come on!"

"Who's that?" Annie asked Shane.

"I dunno. Not sure where it's coming from."

"Sounds angry."

"Yeah, I'll say."

They walked down the ramp to where the Lady J was tied. Shane helped Annie over the gunwale of the boat. Murphy jumped in and immediately started sniffing furiously around the deck.

Moments later they heard the voice again. "Useless piece of crap! Come on!"

Shane looked around and could quickly tell which boat the shouts were emanating from. "I should have guessed." He gestured with his chin towards a rusting, black-hulled trawler at the end of the pier about fifty feet away that Annie had assumed was abandoned.

"Who is it?" Annie asked.

"Johnny Souza. Everybody calls him Souza the Loser because he's such a sad sack. My dad used to say that Johnny has the reverse of the Midas touch, everything he touches turns to shit."

"Souza? Is he related to Chief Souza?"

"I think they're brothers, but I'm not sure. There's a lot of Souzas in Provincetown. My dad knew him, warned me about him actually. Said he's an alcoholic nutcase with a bad temper."

"That's nice," Annie said sarcastically.

"All I know is he's the kind of guy you want to stay away from."

"You don't need to tell me twice. So, he's Billy's uncle?"

"I guess so."

"Must make for interesting holidays."

Johnny Souza stepped out onto the deck of his boat and peered over the stern. He grabbed a long-handled boat hook and appeared to be trying to snag something in the water. As Annie and Shane looked on, they saw him pull up a long piece of black rope that had apparently been caught around his rudder. Johnny turned around and appeared startled to see them watching him.

"You OK?" Shane shouted.

"Yeah, just some friggin' line wrapped around the prop shaft." The cigarette dangling from Johnny's lower lip bounced in cadence with his words. "Lucky I could get it off without having to swim."

"Tell me about it," Shane replied. He had the job more than once of having to don a diver's mask and snorkel to disentangle lobster trap ropes from his propeller shaft.

"If he'd used sinking line, that wouldn't have happened, you know," Annie whispered with a smile.

"Thanks, I'll keep that in mind," Shane said flatly as he started the Lady J's diesel engine. After a few minutes of warming up, he asked Annie to cast off the dock lines that secured the boat. Once they pulled away from the dock, Murphy was at the bow, wagging his tail wildly.

Annie and Shane occupied the vinyl swivel seats in the open cabin. Annie enjoyed the early morning sunshine as they made their way out of the harbor. She turned around to see the pink sunlight reflecting off the white buildings of Provincetown, but her eyes were drawn back to Johnny Souza's decrepit boat. He was standing in the stern with his arms crossed, cigarette still dangling from his lips, watching them head out to sea. Something about the way he watched them gave Annie the creeps. She couldn't put her finger on what it was, but the look in his eyes was clearly one of disapproval.

Chapter 13

By 8:45 a.m., Chief Souza had been at his desk for two hours. He was pouring over the preliminary autopsy report that was faxed from the Barnstable County Coroner's office. Linda Hanscomb had not died from drowning, but from strangulation, as he had suspected. She was probably killed at the Whale Center office, taken to a boat, then dumped at sea. That's a lot of transportation, the chief thought. With any luck, there would be opportunities for evidence as well as witnesses.

The phone on his desk rang. He could see that it was an internal call from the front desk. "Yeah, Carla" he answered.

"Hi, Chief. Mark Ryder is here. He said he'll be doing the press conference with you."

"Right. Send him in. How much time do we have before the press conference?"

"About five minutes."

"OK, Carla, thanks."

He hung up the phone as Mark Ryder, Cape and Islands District Attorney, knocked on the door.

"Morning, Chief," he said cheerfully as he let himself into the office.

"Hi, Mark, come on in." He motioned to a wooden chair in front of his desk.

The sprightly DA dropped his briefcase on the floor and sat. The two had worked together previously on a number of cases over the years ranging from an ecstasy distribution ring in Provincetown's dance clubs to homicides.

"So Mark, what's the latest?"

"I was about to ask you the same. Any suspects yet?"

"There's a girlfriend with a prior murder conviction and an ex-husband who seems like he's hiding something. I'm watching both of them to see if they do anything out of the ordinary."

"Well, you might want to take a look at this" the DA said retrieving a piece of paper from his briefcase. "This is the blood work report on Linda Hanscomb. I think you'll find this interesting."

The chief's eyes narrowed as he read the report, then his jaw dropped as he looked up to a stone faced Mark Ryder. "You've got to be kidding me. What the hell is going on here?"

"I don't know any more than you do, Chief. I think we should sit on this information for now. We don't need to show all of our cards, especially to the press."

"I agree. This is enough of a media circus already. Which reminds me, how do you want to do the press conference?"

"It's your show, Chief. Tell 'em what you want them to know and I'll back you up."

"OK. Let's get going. They're set up outside."

"Yes, I saw them on the way in."

Chief Souza donned his cap and straightened his tie in the small mirror on his wall. As the two stepped outside, they were greeted by a flock of reporters from the Boston and Cape Cod press. Chief Souza had given many press conferences during his tenure and had learned the importance of appearing confident and in control in front of the media. He stepped up to the podium which sprouted a ridiculous crop of over a dozen microphones. Once the reporters quieted down, he spoke:

"Thank you all for coming. I'm Chief Souza of the Provincetown Police Department and this is District Attorney Mark Ryder. Yesterday afternoon at approximately 3:30 pm, the whale watch boat Explorer spotted and retrieved the body of thirty-nine year old Dr. Linda Hanscomb approximately two miles off Race Point. Dr. Hanscomb was a world renowned researcher at the Whale Center, and long time Provincetown resident. She was last seen Thursday night. This department, in cooperation with the Cape and Islands District Attorney's office, has launched an investigation and we are seeking the public's help in this case. If anyone has information about this crime, please call the Provincetown Police Department or the District Attorney's office. I'll now take any questions you might have."

The group of reporters broke into chaotic chatter, shouting questions.

"One at a time," Chief Souza said holding up his hands. "Yes?" He pointed to a buxom bleach blonde in a tailored miniskirt.

"Thanks, Chief. Tina Johnson, Eyewitness 3 news. Do you have any suspects yet in this case?"

"No, we do not. That's why we're asking for the public's cooperation. This is a small town, and we're hoping that somebody either saw or heard something Thursday night that might help us. Yes?" he pointed at another reporter.

"Jim Taylor, Channel 12. How was she killed?"

"The initial autopsy report indicates strangulation. We're still waiting for further reports later today that might give us more information. Yes?"

"Ravi Sharma, Boston Post. How long had her body been in the water?"

"Again, we don't have all of the information yet, but probably about twelve hours. OK, that's it for now. Thank you all.

We'll have another press conference at 5:00 p.m."

"Chief! Chief! Wait a minute! One more question!" shrieked Betsy Gilmore. Before he could refuse, she blurted out "Is there any truth to the rumor that Linda Hanscomb was pregnant?"

The chief looked stunned. He tried to retain his composure as he leaned into the podium. "As I said, we don't have the full autopsy report yet, so we don't know all of Dr. Hanscomb's medical history. I will caution you about rumors and speculation, however. That will not help us solve this murder. Thank you."

As the chief stepped away from the podium, the reporters shouted questions at him. "Is it true? Was she pregnant? Who's the father? I thought she was gay? Chief Souza! Chief Souza!"

Chief Souza stormed down the hall to his office with Mark Ryder five steps behind him. "Close the door," he growled as he sat down in his chair.

"What the hell was that Mark? How did a reporter for the local paper have this report before I did? There's got to be a leak in your office."

"I'm really sorry, Chief. I have no idea how that got out." He paused for a moment while he bit his lip. "Look on the bright side, everyone's going to be paying attention to this case, so, hopefully, you'll get more leads."

"Great. Now this will be a three ring circus with me in the middle. I don't need this."

Chief Souza picked up the preliminary autopsy report and read aloud the section that had caught him by surprise before the press conference.

"Blood tests indicate that the deceased was pregnant. Further investigation suggests that she was carrying a fetus that had been gestating for six to eight weeks." He put the paper down and looked across the table to the DA.

"Tell me, Mark, who would be most likely to kill her, her girlfriend, or the father of the baby?"

"First, you need to figure out who the father is."

"This just got a lot more complicated," the Chief said with a sigh.

The phone on his desk rang again, another internal call.

"Yeah."

"Hi, Chief. A reporter from Inside Edition is on the line. Do you want to talk to him?"

"Tell him the next press conference is at five. I have a lot of work to do, so tell that to any other reporters who call, OK?"

"Right Chief."

"Thanks, Carla" he said while hanging up.

"I need to talk to Mary Ellen Johnson and Bruce Waters. Care to join me?"

"May you live in interesting times," said Mark. That's the ancient Chinese curse, isn't it?"

"Something like that. Come on, let's go." The chief stood and put on his hat. As he did, the phone rang again.

"Yeah?"

"Chief, we just got a report that a neighbor heard gunshots from Mary Ellen Johnson's place. We have officers on the way there now."

"OK, I'm on my way. Thanks, Carla.

Hanging up the phone hurriedly he shouted "Let's go!"

"What's going on?"

"Interesting times. I'll explain it on the way."

Chapter 14

Chief Souza pulled up to the curb in front of Mary Ellen Johnson's house and gallery on Commercial Street. "What's the situation?" he asked Officer McGuire through the lowered window of his Crown Victoria.

"Neighbors heard two or three gunshots around 9:05 this morning, about twenty minutes ago. When we got here, we saw Mary Ellen walking around the house with a handgun, but she won't let anyone in to talk to her and she won't answer the phone."

"She didn't shoot herself?"

"We don't think so. She appears OK."

"Who did she shoot?"

"That we don't know. We haven't gotten an officer close enough to look through the windows yet."

"Do you think we should call the SRT?" asked Mark.

Chief Souza pondered this for a second. The police departments on Cape Cod had a trained regional Special Response Team to call on for potentially dangerous incidents like these. Although they were effective, they were anything but subtle. With all of the media in town already, the last thing he wanted was another event for them to capture on camera.

"No, not yet. I'll try to talk to her and we'll see how this plays out. When was the last time anyone called her?"

"We're calling every two minutes, but she hasn't picked up yet," answered Officer McGuire.

"Have you used the loudspeaker?"

"OK, I'll try that." Flipping the P/A switch on the control panel of his car, Chief Souza picked up the microphone and depressed the call button. "Mary Ellen? This is Chief Souza. I'm worried that somebody might be hurt in there, or that you are going to hurt yourself. I'm going to call you on the phone. I want you to pick up so that I know everybody is safe." He released the call button on the side of the microphone as Officer McGuire placed a cell phone in his free hand.

He placed the phone to his ear and could hear it ringing. With his other hand holding the microphone, he again used the loudspeaker on his car.

"Come on, Mary Ellen, pick up the phone." He could see her moving through the house slowly and raise the phone to her ear.

"Hello?" she said in a quiet voice that sounded very distant.

"Hello Mary Ellen. It's Chief Souza. What's going on?"

"I…I don't know. There's a lot of cops here, outside my house. Am I in trouble? I didn't do anything."

"We had calls from your neighbors saying they heard gunshots from inside your house. Did you shoot anyone?"

"Just the damn television, with all the trash talking about Linda."

"You shot the television?"

"That's right. Lucky I wasn't there, I'd shoot that bitch reporter, too," she said with a chuckle.

Chief Souza knew this wasn't the time to admit that the same thought had crossed his mind. "Mary Ellen, I need you to listen to me. I need you to put the gun down and come outside so we can talk. Can you do that?"

"We're talking now, aren't we?"

"Yes, yes we are. But I want to see that you are all right. Have you taken any drugs or alcohol?"

"Not really. I had a few drinks last night to settle me down."

This confirmed the Chief's suspicion. She was probably drinking all night.

"OK, listen. Put down the gun and walk toward the front door. Can you do that for me?"

"I don't want to go to jail."

He could hear the rising hysteria in her voice. "You're not going to jail. We just need to make sure that you're safe."

"You cops are lying. You're always lying. Is Annie there? I want to talk to Annie."

The chief could now see Mary Ellen clearly through the kitchen window. She was pacing around like a crazed animal in a cage. As she passed by the sliding glass door in the dining room that led out to the patio, he could see that she was carrying a small, shiny revolver. Probably a .38, he thought.

"Annie's not here, Mary Ellen. We can talk this out, though, just us. Can you put the gun down?"

As he said that, Mary Ellen raised the gun to her head and screamed into the phone, "I want to talk to Annie, goddamn it! I mean it! Put her on the phone!"

"OK, OK, hold on. I'll try to get Annie on the phone and you can talk to her. OK?"

Chief Souza unclipped his own cell phone from his belt, and scrolled through a list of calls to retrieve Annie's call from last night. Finding it, he pressed the send button.

"I want to talk to her now!" Mary Ellen screamed loud enough to be heard outside.

"OK, hold on, hold on. I'm going to hand the phone to Officer McGuire, just for a minute, OK? Don't hang up."

But as he finished his sentence, he heard the line go dead.

Annie had her hand on the throttle of the Lady J. They had a system worked out. Shane would snag a lobster trap with a boat hook, haul it up through the winch, flip it open to retrieve the lobsters, pick out any spider crabs that got inside, refill the bait bag with a chunk of mackerel, and then close the trap and slide it off the stern into the water. Each trap took Shane about forty five seconds. Annie's job was to keep the boat moving at three miles per hour, just above idle speed, and follow the line of green and yellow buoys in the water that marked Shane's traps. She was amazed that he was able to do this by himself. Each time she came out with him, she became more aware of the many inherent dangers of commercial lobstering.

The phone ringing in her hip pocket startled her. With the tranquility of the calm water and the warm sunshine, she was annoyed that anyone would interrupt the peace of her day. She flipped the phone open, but her caller ID only said Private Caller. Annie noticed that the low battery warning was flashing, and she immediately regretted not charging the phone overnight.

"Hello?" she said.

"Hello, Annie Macalister?"

"Yes, who is this?"

"Chief Souza. Sorry to bother you, but this is an emergency."

Annie's heart started to race.

"Mary Ellen Johnson has barricaded herself in her house and is threatening to hurt herself. She has a handgun and has fired shots already this morning."

"Oh, my god. Are you serious?"

"I'm afraid so. She's asking to speak to you. You've got to help us out."

"Who is it?" Shane called out.

"Hold on Chief" Annie put a hand over the phone. "It's Chief Souza. Mary Ellen's gone crazy or something. She has a gun and she wants to talk to me."

"Oh man, I told you she was trouble," Shane said as he splashed another lobster trap into Cape Cod Bay.

"OK, Chief. What should I do?"

"Can you get down here to Commercial Street?"

"I don't think so. I'm out on Shane's boat right now. We're about a mile off Sesuit Harbor in Dennis. It'll take at least an hour for us to get back."

"I understand. Could you call her? She needs to talk to you for reassurance. I'm trying to get her to put the gun down and come out without hurting herself or any of my officers. I suspect she's been drinking or using drugs. This is potentially a very dangerous situation, I don't suppose you've ever done anything like this before?"

"No," she replied. She understood that he was placing Mary Ellen's and possibly other people's lives in her hands. "Look, Chief, I'm just a college student studying whales, not a hostage negotiator. Are you sure about this?"

"Right now I'm not sure about anything, but she is asking for you. If this doesn't work, I'm going to have send people in after her, and I don't want to do that."

Annie thought for a moment. "OK, I'll do it."

"Great. Thank you. I'm going to hang up, and let Mary Ellen know you'll call. Give me about thirty seconds, then call her, OK?"

"OK. Um, what should I say?"

"Just keep her talking and try to get her to put the gun down."

"OK, I'll do my best. So, I'll just wait a few seconds then call her, right?"

"That's all you need to do. That should buy us some time. Thanks Annie."

"Sure. Good luck, Chief."

Annie lowered the phone and pressed the button to end the call.

"Shane, I'm going to need you to drive for a while."

He looked annoyed at having his work routine broken. "I kinda figured that. So, what are you going to say to her?"

"I have absolutely no idea." Annie scrolled through her list of cell phone numbers and found Mary Ellen's home number. With Shane steering the boat to the next line of lobster traps, she pressed the send button.

The phone rang once, twice, three times. "Please, Mary Ellen, pick up. Don't do this to me."

On the fourth ring, Mary Ellen answered the phone.

"Annie? Is that you?"

"Yes, it's me. Mary Ellen, what are you doing? The chief said you shot a gun in your house? They think you're going to hurt someone, or yourself."

"I'm not going to hurt anyone. I'm just really pissed off."

"Everybody's upset about Linda, Mary Ellen. I can't believe she's gone either."

"That's not the whole of it, Annie. Did you see the news this morning?"

"No, I'm out on Shane's boat. We've been out since six o'clock."

"Remember that damn reporter from yesterday?"

"Oh, the one on the bike? The one that looked like the wicked witch of the west."

"Yeah, that one. She announced at the news conference that Linda was pregnant."

Annie was momentarily stunned into silence. "What? Pregnant? How is that possible? Is it true?"

"Yeah, it is. We wanted to have a baby, so we got a sperm donor back in June."

"Are you serious? I had no idea."

Neither did Chief Souza, who had tapped into Mary Ellen's phone line so that he could hear the call. .

"Well, we'd been talking about it for a while. Linda was the healthier of us, so we decided that she would be the one to carry the baby. Now I've lost everything, Annie."

"I, I don't know what to say Mary Ellen. I'm so sorry." As Annie listened to the silence on the line, she wished she could be there to comfort her. "Mary Ellen, do you still have the gun?"

"Yeah, I guess I overreacted."

"I think it's time you put it down before someone gets hurt. There's been enough hurting around here the past few days."

"You're right Annie, No more hurting. This needs to be over with. Now. Goodbye Annie, thanks for all your help."

"Wait a minute, Mary Ellen. Don't hang up. Put down the gun and go outside. Mary Ellen, are you still there?"

Annie didn't get her answer. Instead, she heard popping sound that sounded like a firecracker. Then her phone beeped twice and the battery went dead.

"Oh my God, Shane. I think I just killed Mary Ellen."

Chapter 15

Angus Black could have been enjoying himself had he not been on a mission to kill a man. He rose early and left the Bangor hotel room before dawn. At 9:30 he parked his car in a garage in downtown Boston across the street from the dock where the Provincetown Fast Ferry departed. He tried to blend in, dressing casually in a baseball hat, dark sunglasses, khaki pants, and a blue Polo shirt. Clutched firmly in his right hand was a Louis Vuitton leather bag containing $5,000 in cash, a change of clothes, and a 9mm Glock pistol. He liked the utility of this gun, as it was lightweight, with a carbon-fiber body, a generous 18-round clip, and a smooth action. The first time he fired it he realized why it had become the sidearm of choice for police departments throughout the United States.

He stood in line at the ticket booth next to the New England Aquarium along with a congregation of Boston's young gay and lesbian professionals who were on their way to Provincetown for a long weekend of partying. This is certainly a jovial crowd, Angus thought to himself. Too bad my visit is for business, not pleasure.

"One ticket for the 11:00 a.m. boat, please," Angus said to the young woman inside the Fast Ferry booth.

"One way or round trip?"

"Round trip."

"$61.95, with the tax. Cash or charge?"

"Cash." Angus pulled a crisp $100 bill out of the money clip in his pocket.

"Here's your change, and your ticket. Have a nice weekend."

"Thanks."

Angus moved from the ticket counter to the waiting line on the dock. There were already about fifty people milling about, many talking on cell phones and drinking expensive lattes from the Starbucks across the street. Angus surveyed the crowd and the surrounding area trying to get a sense of any security measures that might be in place.

There were cameras atop a nearby hotel as well as on the parking garage where he left his car. These made him a bit uneasy, as they would have a record of him coming and going. Of course, this would only be a problem if he were to become a suspect which he did not intend to be. He would simply act the part of a tourist in town for the weekend, then slip out on the 9:00 a.m. boat the following morning.

What Angus was really on the lookout for was a metal detector. Even though the Glock's body was composite plastic, there was enough steel inside the barrel and firing mechanism to set off a magnetometer. Seeing none, however, he relaxed for a moment and lit a Dunhill cigarette while he waited to board the boat.

At 10:50, the gate was opened for passengers to board. Many went directly to the bar to get an early start on their weekend frolic. Angus made his way to the bow, where he had a good view of Boston Harbor and Logan International Airport.

Precisely at 11:00 a.m., the dock lines were cast off and the ship's whistle blew a short, deafening blast. It was a beautiful sunny day and Angus was looking forward to the ninety-minute trip across Cape Cod Bay to Provincetown. He was careful not to let his guard down, as he fully understood the serious nature of his business.

Hopefully, by tomorrow morning, he thought to himself, this whole sordid affair would be over and I could go back to what I really do best, making a profit for myself and my shareholders.

As the ferry passed the Long Point Lighthouse that marked the entrance to Provincetown Harbor, it came parallel to a white lobster boat. Angus made out the name "Lady J" in blue paint on the bow. Some of the passengers on the ferry were waiving to the man and woman on board, trying to get them to wave back or at least smile. They didn't. They just solemnly stared ahead as they made their way to the opposite side of MacMillan Wharf.

Chapter 16

Shane nudged the Lady J into her slip at MacMillan Wharf. Annie could tell that he was annoyed that he had to return to the dock before finishing his work, but she didn't care. She needed to find out what happened to Mary Ellen.

They hadn't spoken since they started to head back in an hour ago. Shane was grumbling about wasting his day and fuel and only pulling a handful of lobster traps. Once he ran the engine up to full throttle, any conversation was impossible. Anyway, what was there to say? Annie felt that she had been tested and that she failed miserably. Shane, obviously, didn't sense this, or worse yet, if he did, he didn't show a hint of compassion towards her.

As soon as the hull of the boat bumped against the crinkled fire hose nailed to the side of the floating dock, Annie sprang over the gunwale and started up the gangway to the pier.

"Annie, wait a minute. Where are you going?"

"I've got to go see if Mary Ellen is OK."

"Want me to come with you?"

"No, I'll be all right by myself."

"I'll call you later."

"Whatever. I've got to go."

Annie was quietly fuming to herself as she bounded up to the pier. "Want me to come with you…" she muttered to herself. "Of course I do, jerk! You're my boyfriend and I just got someone killed. Jesus, what am I doing with him?"

Annie stormed through the crowd that had disembarked from the ferry. All around her were people greeting each other with hugs and handshakes. The only thing Annie could think of was getting to Mary Ellen's house as quickly as she could. Tourists rolling suitcases and chatting on cell phones jostled her as she made her way down the wharf.

Annie bumped into a middle aged woman with a close cropped mullet and tattoos on her arms.

"Hey, watch it!" the woman snarled.

"Sorry," Annie said meekly. Turning around, she didn't see the suitcase at her feet, and before she realized what was happening, she had the brief sensation of flying before landing hard on the hot concrete roadway.

Annie's head was spinning as she lay there. A crowd of people stood around her, staring, until she heard a man's voice with a deep Scottish accent.

"Are you OK?" the stranger asked as he extended a hand to help her up.

"Yeah, but I feel like a complete idiot."

"That was a nasty fall. Are you sure you're not hurt?"

"I'm fine, thanks. Ouch! Oh, my knee!"

"You're bleeding. Come on, let me help you over to that bench."

"That's very nice of you, really I'm fine."

"It's the least I can do. Anyway, it would be ungentlemanly to leave you bleeding in the middle of the street after all." With one arm around Annie's shoulder, the stranger helped Annie hobble over to a bench under a shade tree.

"I'm Thomas. Thomas Lawrence. And you are?"

"Annie Macalister. Thanks for your help, Mr. Lawrence."

The stranger smiled and said, "Call me Tom."

"OK, Tom."

For the first time since she fell, Annie actually looked at the stranger who helped her up. He was handsome, trim and fit, with silver hair. She'd never been attracted to older men, but there was something vaguely Sean Connery about him that she found mesmerizing.

Angus recognized her name instantly. He'd read about her on the Whale Center website. Luck favors the prepared mind, he thought.

"Where were you going in such a hurry, Annie?"

"I've got to go see a friend. I think she needs help. Oh, hey, officer!"

Annie waved to a pair of Provincetown police officers riding by on mountain bikes. They wheeled around and stopped abruptly before her and Angus Black.

"You all right Miss? Your knee looks pretty bad."

"I think so. Do you have any bandages?"

"Sure, hold on."

Officer Roger Davenport put down the kickstand on his bike and unzipped a black bag hanging under the seat which contained, among other things, a first aid kit for situations like this one.

"What's your name?" Officer Davenport asked as he kneeled on the pavement to attend to Annie's wounded knee.

"Annie. Annie Macalister."

"You're Annie Macalister? Hey, Chief Souza is looking for you. He wanted to thank you for your help this morning with Mary Ellen Johnson."

"Thank me? I thought I got her killed."

"No way, you saved her life."

"But I heard a gunshot over the phone, I know I did."

"Well, that's true. You kept her talking on the phone long enough for the chief to take her down with a beanbag. She was raising the gun to her head when he did it."

"A beanbag?"

"Yes. It's a beanbag about two inches square, fired from a shotgun. It hits with a lot of impact, but doesn't usually do any permanent damage."

"So, Mary Ellen's OK?"

"She'll be sore for a while, that's for sure. Maybe a broken rib, but she's not hurt otherwise."

"Where is she? Can I go and see her?"

"I'm afraid not, Miss. She was taken to Cape Cod Hospital for treatment and she's being held on charges."

"Charges? What charges?"

"For now, it's illegal possession of a handgun. I really can't tell you any more than that. But, I'm sure the chief can fill you in on the rest. Anyhow, he wants to thank you for your help. OK, that looks better. How's your knee feel?"

"Better, thanks. Listen, officer, I'm glad Mary Ellen's OK, but is she being charged for Linda Hanscomb's murder?"

Officer Davenport sighed, "Like I said, I can't tell you any more. I'm not even sure myself what's going on. But if you call the chief, he might be able to say."

Angus was standing over the two, absorbing every word of the conversation. He was also re-evaluating the objectives of his mission.

"Annie," he said, "why don't you let me buy you a drink while you rest your knee for a little while?"

"That sounds like a good idea," said Officer Davenport "Go and relax a bit. You've had a tough day."

Annie thought about it for a split second. She wasn't in the habit of letting strangers buy her drinks. He seems like a nice enough guy for helping me, and my knee is still throbbing. Besides, Mary Ellen is fifty miles away in the hospital, and there isn't anything she could do for her now. "Okay. Just one, though."

"Ah, that's the spirit." Angus extended a hand to help her up.

"How about over there?" Annie pointed to the Surf Club at the end of MacMillan Wharf. She knew it was on the expensive side, but it had a nice view of the harbor, and she also knew Shane would never see her there.

"Looks fine. Come on, now, let me help you."

"Thanks Tom. You're very kind."

"It's the least I can do," Angus smirked.

Angus escorted Annie across the street and held the door for her when they arrived at the Surf Club. The cool blast of air conditioning produced a wave of goose bumps on Annie's skin. The restaurant was still busy from the summer lunch crowd, but they found a table for two in the corner near the window. Angus held her chair as she sat. Quite the charming gentleman Annie thought.

"So, what brings you to Provincetown?" Annie asked.

"Just a weekend holiday. Plus, there's a friend of mine over here I haven't seen in a while."

"Oh, a friend. I understand."

"Ah, I know what you're thinking. It's not like that. He's just a business associate. Anyway, if I were gay and in Provincetown for the weekend, why would I be buying a pretty lady like you a drink?"

"Good point," Annie said blushing.

A waiter appeared at the table. "Hi, welcome to the Surf Club. My name's Adam, I'll be your server. Can I get you started with drinks?"

"I'll have a Grey Goose martini with a twist." Angus replied confidently.

"Fabulous, and for the lady?"

"That sounds good. I'll have the same."

"OK, can I see some ID please?"

Embarrassed, Annie retrieved her driver's license from the back pocket of her shorts.

"Perfect," said Adam, first scrutinizing then handing Annie back her license "I'll get those two Grey Goose martinis right up for you."

"Thank you very much," Angus turned his gaze back to Annie. "Now what's this about a murder?"

"Oh, it's awful. My supervisor at work was found murdered

yesterday. It looks like she was strangled, then thrown in the ocean from a boat. I actually found her and helped drag her on board. I didn't know it was her at first, she was so bloated."

Angus feigned compassion. "That's terrible. Do the police have any idea who did it?"

"Her girlfriend's been arrested and I bet they'll charge her with the murder. I didn't think she did it at first, but she's just gone nuts since Linda died. She tried to kill herself this morning. That's what that cop was talking about."

"Sounds like she couldn't live with the guilt."

Annie thought about this for a moment, then replied, "No, I guess she couldn't."

"Here are your martinis." The waiter placed the drinks on the table. "Can I get you two anything else?"

Angus looked across the table at Annie, who was staring blankly out the window. "No. That's all."

"OK, enjoy."

"Here's to old friends and new friendships." Angus offered.

They clinked glasses.

"Oh, that's strong," Annie said with an exhale.

"But smooth. So tell me Annie, what do you think happened? Was it a lover's quarrel that got out of hand?"

"I don't know. Linda's office was ransacked that night. I talked to the Chief of Police here, and he thought it looked like a break in at first."

"Maybe the girlfriend, what's her name?"

"Mary Ellen," Annie replied as she took another sip.

"Maybe Mary Ellen wanted it to look that way to cover her tracks. Besides, what would anyone want from her office? Was there money there or something?"

"Oh no. No money. We work at a whale research program. Money's the last thing we'd have lying around. Linda and I were working on a project that could stop oil and gas drilling on Stellwagen Bank, just offshore of Provincetown."

Angus was intrigued by her words. "Interesting. How would you stop it?"

"Well, the area around Stellwagen Bank is the primary feeding ground for many species of whales, including the North Atlantic Right Whale. They're the most endangered whale in the world. The best we can estimate, their total population is between three and four hundred in the world."

"That's all?"

"Yeah, that's it. So anything that can be done to save their feeding habitat is crucial for the survival of the whole species."

"How does this affect oil and gas exploration?" Angus realized that he was getting exactly the information he wanted from her.

"Stellwagen Bank is a shallow area of water. The construction and ships that would be needed for exploration there would pretty much guarantee fatal collisions with whales. Every right whale that gets killed just brings the entire species closer to extinction. The Endangered Species Act says that you can't knowingly disturb or threaten any endangered animal."

Angus decided to play dumb to see how much Annie knew. So far, it seemed like she knew quite a lot.

"Is there that much oil out there to make it profitable?"

"There probably is. The Canadians are already drilling for natural gas off of Nova Scotia. Apparently, there's enough there that they're building new drilling rigs."

"Well, Annie. This is all very interesting. I see you've finished your drink, would you like another?"

"No, thanks, I really should get going. I haven't been home since yesterday and I need to talk to the chief about Linda's murder. You know, now that I've been talking to you, I really don't think that Mary Ellen killed her."

"You don't?" Angus asked with some alarm.

"No. I think whoever killed Linda wanted to stop this report from being filed. She was supposed to go to Washington, D.C. in a few weeks to present the findings to the EPA. We were hoping that they would enact a permanent ban on oil and gas exploration in the entire Gulf of Maine."

Angus could feel his palms begin to sweat. "So you're suggesting some kind of conspiracy with the oil companies? Come on, now. You can't be serious."

"Exactly. That's exactly it. I just have to find a way to prove it now. Oh, thanks Tom. Thanks for everything. I've got to go find Chief Souza."

"With your knee like that? Let me call my friend and he can give you a ride. He needs to pick me up anyway."

"Oh, thanks, but I'm OK, really."

When Annie stood, her feet felt a little unsteady on account of the martini and her injured knee.

Angus left $25 on the table to cover the two drinks. He

followed her to the door, thinking of a way that he could capture her without causing a scene. He felt a twinge of guilt. *She seems like a nice, if naïve, girl,* he thought. *It's a shame really, but she needs to be silenced too.*

Annie stepped out into the brightness and heat of the midday July sun. As she did, she saw Juicy Freeman running by with a large backpack and a ten-foot aluminum pole.

"Juicy, what's going on?"

"Hey, Annie mon. We lookin' fo' you. Bruce say there's a whale stuck in fishing nets off Truro. We're headin' out now. You comin?"

Annie had been out on a few whale entanglement rescues this summer. There had been many others, but Linda Hanscomb and Bruce Waters were on the first response team. Now without Linda, they were shorthanded.

Without hesitation, she answered, "Yeah, Juicy. I'm coming. Tell Bruce I'll be there in a minute." Turning to Angus she said, "Well Tom, that's what I'm here to do. It's what Linda would want. Thanks for the drink, but I've got to go."

The smell of citrus and vodka hung in the air as she kissed him lightly on the cheek. Angus was speechless. He was not used to affection, especially from someone he was planning to kill.

"Right, well, um, good luck then."

"Thanks Tom, I'll see you around. If not, enjoy your weekend."

"I'm sure I'll see you again," Angus muttered as he watched Annie hobble as quickly as she could down MacMillan Wharf to the Whale Center's rescue boat. "Sooner than you might think."

Chapter 17

Annie arrived at the dock as Juicy was stowing the supply backpack and poles that are used to remove fishing gear from an entangled whale. She glanced over to the other side of MacMillan Wharf where the fishing boats tie up and noticed that the Lady J was not in her slip. Apparently, Shane had gone back out to finish his day's work. She couldn't blame him, but she was still upset about his cold treatment after the incident with Mary Ellen. Sometimes he would pout like a little boy when things didn't go exactly his way and she was getting tired of it.

"Annie, what happened to your knee?" Bruce Waters asked.

"Oh, it's OK. I tripped over some tourist's luggage and skinned it."

"Juicy told me he ran into you. I'm glad you're coming along. This isn't a two-person job."

Annie felt the sadness in his voice. Linda and Bruce were a dedicated team when it came to working directly with the whales. Annie had assisted them before on whale rescues and she could see that, even though Linda and Bruce were no longer married, they had almost a telepathic communication.

"I'm glad I can help. What do need me to do?"

"We're just about ready. Juicy's got the bow line ready. Why don't you untie us from the stern."

"OK." Annie walked to the rear of the thirty-eight foot vessel. Originally used by the Coast Guard to chase drug runners in the Caribbean, it combined the light weight of an inflatable boat with a high performance Kevlar hull. With two 225 horsepower outboard motors, the rescue boat could easily top sixty miles per hour. Everything about this boat excited Annie. It was like riding in a fast sports car with the top down.

"Lines clear?" Bruce hollered.

"Bow clear," Juicy replied.

"Stern clear," Annie shouted.

Bruce moved the throttle from neutral to reverse, and eased the boat away from the floating dock that it shared with the Explorer which was out on a whale watch. Annie coiled the dock line and hung it on a cleat. She hadn't had much experience around boats before this summer, but now she estimated that she had spent nearly 400 hours at sea since May.

"So, where are we headed?" Annie asked Bruce.

"About a mile off of the Golf Ball in Truro." he replied, using the local nickname for the Federal Aviation Administration radar dome in North Truro. "A tuna boat reported a large finback with gear entangled around its mouth and fin. Apparently, there's floats on it, and the whale's having a tough time diving."

"Do you think it's lobster gear?"

"Probably. When they dive for food in these shallow waters, a lot of times the ropes connecting the lobster traps get caught in their jaws. Sometimes they just work themselves loose, but this one sounds pretty bad."

"How long will it take to get out there?"

"Once we get out of the harbor, it'll only take about half an hour."

Annie's heart was racing with excitement but, at the same time, it was full of sadness. Forty-eight hours ago, Linda would have been standing next to Bruce at the helm of the rescue boat. She would instinctively know what to do, which tools to use, and how to stay safe while working around an injured ninety foot animal. Before, Annie had only watched from the boat and helped to videotape the rescue.

She had never quite figured out the relationship between Bruce Waters and Linda Hanscomb. Annie knew that they had been married at one time, before Linda and Mary Ellen started seeing each other. When they argued about policies or budgets at the Whale Center, they certainly sounded like a married couple, but it was clear that each had a vital role in the organization that helped the entire place run efficiently. Bruce was a master salesman and fundraiser, Linda had a scientific mind, able to explain the most complex theories in a way that anyone could understand. Annie held both of them in the highest regard. She wondered to herself how Bruce was coping with Linda being gone.

Just as she was trying to find the words to ask him, Bruce shook his head and said, "I don't know what I'm going to do without her. I'm numb Annie, just numb. Even though we haven't been married for years now, she was still my best friend. I don't know how I'll get by, or the center for that matter. I'm just trying to deal with one thing at a time. I spent all morning making arrangements for a memorial service tomorrow afternoon."

"Where's that going to be?" Annie had been wondering what, if any, plans had been made.

"At the Unitarian Church on Commercial Street at one o'clock. She always liked that church."

"Do you need any help?"

"No, thanks. It's all set. I know the minister there, though I haven't been to church in a long time. It's just a time to get together and remember her."

"Will there be a funeral?"

"No, she wanted to be cremated and her ashes scattered at

sea, so that's what we'll do. That won't be until sometime next week. We'll take the Explorer, so there is room for everybody that wants to come."

"I'm so sorry." Annie gently placed her hand on top of Bruce's for a moment.

"Thanks." He pulled his hand away to wipe a tear from under his sunglasses.

For the next half hour, the three rescuers did not speak, partly because the boat was skipping over the waves at forty miles per hour, but mostly because nobody knew what else there was to say.

Annie kept her eye on the GPS map in the console of the boat. The whale's last known coordinates were locked in and the graphic display showed their boat closing rapidly on that spot. As the FAA radar dome in North Truro came into view, Bruce seemed to have composed himself. He spoke with an authoritative and professional demeanor.

"All right, keep your eyes open for spouts. We're pretty close to where it was last seen."

The three of them scanned the horizon for the telltale spray of a whale's exhalation. Annie and Juicy looked through binoculars, while Bruce kept one hand on the wheel and eased the throttle back with the other.

"I see it!" Annie shouted. Ten hours a day of whale watching for the past two and a half months had made her eyes very sharp when it came to finding whales. "Looks like a finback." She pointed in the direction of the spout and Bruce turned the boat to where she was pointing.

"How far out?" Bruce asked.

"About two miles."

"Hang on."

Annie and Juicy immediately grabbed hold of something secure as Bruce pushed the throttle all the way forward. Bruce loved the speed of this boat, and he wasn't afraid to use it. The boat quickly accelerated. He flipped a switch on the dash that dropped the trim tabs lower into the water which made the bow drop down so that it was parallel with the horizon. They closed the gap between their location and the sighted whale in less than three minutes.

Bruce dropped the boat into idle when they came within one hundred feet of the whale so they could survey the animal.

"It's a finback all right. Big one, too. About seventy-five feet, eh Bruce?" Juicy observed.

"I'd say so, Juice."

"Looks like the ropes are around the mouth and head," Annie said while looking through her binoculars. "Those lines have been there for a while. Look how the area around the blowhole is all infected and raw. This is a very sick animal."

"All right, here's what we'll do," Bruce announced. "We'll come around behind the whale and try to secure some buoys to the gear she's dragging. That'll slow her down and might help pull some of the gear off. If that doesn't work, we'll use a Zodiac to get real close and try to cut the lines off by hand. Each of you grab a boat hook and try to find a piece of line that we can tie the buoy to."

Bruce maneuvered the boat close to the enormous mammal's tail. The twin 4-stroke outboard motors were nearly silent at slow speeds. Experience had taught him that so long as they moved slowly the whale would sense that they were not a threat.

Annie couldn't help but think about yesterday when she and Juicy were standing side by side with boat hooks in their hands, just like they were now. Could that have only been yesterday? It seemed like a lifetime ago. The image of Linda's body lying on the deck of the Explorer was forever burned into her memory.

Juicy's voice snapped Annie back to the task at hand.

"C'mon, Annie, grab it!"

Annie stretched out her boat hook and snagged one of the pieces of rope that was trailing behind the whale's fluke.

"Got it!"

"All right," Bruce shouted, "get the telemetry buoy on it, quick!"

Annie held the rope while Juicy clamped a buoy equipped with a GPS transmitter, strobe light, and a radar reflector.

"Hurry up, Juice, I feel like I'm taking a forty-ton dog for a walk here."

"Almost done, Annie. OK, that's it, let it go."

Annie dropped the line back into the water, relieved to be let loose from the powerful creature. "Now what?" she asked.

"Well, now that we've got the telemetry buoy on, we'll shorten the lines she's dragging. Then, we'll try to attach some larger floating buoys to slow her down and try to drag some of those lines off."

"We need to get those ropes off of her head, they're definitely blocking the blowhole," yelled Annie.

"I know, we will," Bruce replied confidently.

The three rescuers worked silently. Each one snagged whatever dangling ropes they could with a boat hook and cut off as much as possible. Then, they attached a large, bright orange buoy to slow the whale down.

Bruce looked dismayed after an hour of working. "It's not enough drag to pull the ropes off. They're only getting tighter. We need to attach a parachute. Juicy, get the Zodiac ready."

"OK, Bruce." Juicy went to the bow and started to untie the twelve foot inflatable boat.

"Parachute?" Annie asked.

"It's a small parachute that will slow her down so that we can cut those lines. They don't like it much and sometimes they get a little itchy."

"Itchy?" Annie was not comforted by the idea of being next to a forty-ton animal with a bad attitude.

"These creatures are used to doing what they want without much interference," Bruce explained calmly. "When they feel all the floats and parachutes pulling against them they can panic. Kind of like the first time a horse gets saddled. They can't swim away, they can't dive, so they're likely to thrash their tails or breech right out the water to try to shake it all loose. It can get a little hairy. So, do you want to cut or drive?"

"What do you mean?"

"I mean, do you want to help cut the lines or drive the boat? It's your call, but we're short-handed and we need two in the Zodiac and one to drive."

Annie thought it over for a second. This is what she had always wanted to do since hearing about the Whale Center's work in college.

"I want to help cut lines."

"I was hoping you'd say that. You'll need a life vest and a helmet. There should be some your size in the locker." Bruce pointed to a box built into the floor of the boat.

"Everything's ready!" Juicy called out.

"Good. I need you to drive, Juice, Annie and I are going in the Zodiac."

"OK, Mon."

Annie opened the hatch and saw four lacrosse helmets with wire mesh facemasks. She picked up the first and tried it on, but it was far too big. On the next one, she noticed a name written on the inside in black marker, L. Hanscom.

"Oh my god, Bruce, this was Linda's, and it fits just right."

"Really? Well, wear it then. She was the best there was at this."

Annie put the helmet on and buckled the chin strap. She felt proud to be able to take Linda's place on a rescue, but was nervous about the task ahead. As she zipped up her flotation vest, she heard her grandmother's voice in her head saying "You can do this." She whispered the words to herself. "You can do this, you can do this."

Her whisper must have been louder than she realized because Bruce laid his hand gently on her shoulder and said, "I know you can. I wouldn't have asked you if I didn't think you were up to the job. Are you ready?"

"I guess so. Just tell me what to do."

"No problem. Let's go."

Bruce swung his legs over the side of the boat and lowered himself into the Zodiac. He reached up and took Annie's hand to help her. Once they were both in, Bruce primed the gas on the outboard motor and pulled the starting cord. After the second pull, it whirred to life.

"Be careful, you two," Juicy yelled from the deck of the rescue boat.

"Thanks, Juice. All set, Annie?"

Annie's fear had been replaced by excitement. "All set, let's do this one for Linda."

With that, Bruce twisted the throttle on the motor, and they buzzed around the struggling whale with nothing to protect them but an inflatable boat and a pair of lacrosse helmets.

Chapter 18

Angus strode across the intersection at the end of MacMillan Wharf to a payphone. He picked up the receiver and punched in ten numbers from a slip of paper he'd retrieved from his pocket.

"Hello?" the voice on the line answered.

"It's me. I'm in Provincetown, and we need to meet."

"What are you doing here?"

"I'm here to clean up the mess you caused. Where are you now?"

"I'm out on my boat. I won't be back until tonight."

"You keep your boat at MacMillan Wharf, right?"

"Yeah, on the commercial pier. Do you have my money?"

"You'll be paid when the job is finished. That's our deal. Meet me at your boat at ten tonight," he growled, slamming down the receiver.

Angus glanced at his Rolex and saw that it was only one o'clock in the afternoon. He stepped into the tourist information center next to a place that sold foot-long hot dogs and looked for a map of Provincetown.

"Can I help you sir?" a perky teenager said.

Angus looked her up and down. He guessed her to be about nineteen, with curly brown hair that fell just past her shoulders. She wore a white polo shirt and tight-fitting khaki shorts that accentuated the graceful form of her legs. Just above her left breast was a pinned-on badge that was imprinted with the

Provincetown Chamber of Commerce logo, and the name Wendy.

"Yes, um, Wendy," Angus said as he leaned in to steal a closer look at her breasts. "I hope you can. I've just arrived in town and will be meeting a friend later tonight, but I have the afternoon free. I'm hoping you can provide me with a map and maybe a few sightseeing suggestions."

"Oh, sure. First let me get you a map." She turned around and walked to the counter in the back. Angus watched as Wendy's shorts swayed rhythmically from side to side. He noticed a small butterfly tattoo on her ankle. Angus nearly got caught staring as she turned and approached him.

"Here you are. Now, depending on what you're looking for, there's lots to do. If you like art galleries, just go out onto Commercial Street and turn right. Walk about ten minutes and you'll be in the East End. There's lots of galleries there. If you turn left, you'll find all kinds of other shops and restaurants. There's a shuttle bus that can take you out to the beaches, too. Is there anything else you'd like to see while you're here?"

Angus repressed what he was really thinking. Wendy stood so close to him that he could feel the heat of her body.

"There is one thing. I've heard about the Whale Center here in Provincetown. Where is that?"

"Sure, let me circle it for you." Wendy pulled a pen out of the front pocket of her shorts. "Just go left onto Commercial Street and keep going until you get past all the restaurants. It will be a residential area of old houses. Their building is right next to the Coast Guard Station." She lowered her voice and said, "but I think they're probably closed today."

"Why is that?" Angus queried.

"It's really sad. One of the biologists there died. The police said she was murdered."

"Murder? That's terrible," Angus said as a twinge of remorse made his stomach muscles tighten.

"Everybody in town is talking about it. No one can believe that something like that would happen here. Sorry to bum you out. I'm sure you'll have a good time here."

"I'm sure I will. Thanks for your help."

"Have a nice day!" Wendy chirped as Angus stepped outside into the bright sunshine.

He walked to Commercial Street, which was jammed with tourists. He felt drawn to see where the murder took place, maybe he could then understand how things went so terribly wrong. He walked on the one side of the street which provided some shade from the glaring sun overhead. He passed countless shops selling everything from fudge to T-shirts with witty messages, such as "Nobody knows I'm Gay!!!" and "Jesus is coming, look busy!"

One store in particular caught his eye. The sign on the front said they carried military surplus and collectables. Angus went in, hoping to find some British insignia from his old regiment. He passed through the cramped racks of new and used fatigues, and eventually found himself in the back of the store facing an entire wall covered with swords, knives, and medieval looking weaponry of every description. This was his kind of place.

His eyes were drawn to a glass display case full of knives. Some were for obvious practical uses, and contained screwdrivers, bottle openers and pull-out tweezers. Suddenly, his eyes lit up with what he saw.

"Excuse me, could I see this one, please?" Angus said to the man behind the counter.

"This one?" The clerk held up a long, thin stiletto. "This has a thumb latch, it opens as quick as a switchblade, but it's like, totally legal."

Angus smiled. Considering what he had in mind, he was not very concerned with the legality of the knife's opening mechanism. "May I try it?"

"Sure." The clerk pressed a button on the side which released the lock on the blade, then folded it into its handle. "Here you are."

"Thanks." Angus was surprised by the lightness of the knife. Holding it in his right hand, he placed his thumb against the latch on the blade and pushed it forward. It snapped open in a split second and securely locked into place. The long, thin blade reflected the sunlight from the skylights overhead. He tested the blade by shaving a few hairs off the back of his arm, which it did effortlessly.

"This will do nicely. How much?"

"$19.95, plus tax."

"That's all?" Angus said as he peeled a few bills from the roll in his pocket.

The clerk handed him his change. "Would you like a bag for that?"

"No thanks." Angus turned to leave the store, his newest weapon clinking lightly against the change in his pocket.

He noticed an antique Union Jack hanging from the ceiling above him. When he looked up at it, he also noticed a security camera trained on the cash register at the knife counter which had obviously recorded his entire transaction. "Damn," he muttered. Angus discretely pulled his baseball cap lower to cover his eyes and quickly made his way to the door where he was able to disappear once again into the throng on Commercial Street.

There was no use feeling angry with himself, Angus reasoned. His mission needed to continue. As long as he didn't draw attention to himself he should be able to cover his tracks and find out how the Whale Center report could impact his business prospects.

After walking for about ten more minutes, Angus saw two Provincetown police cars and a blue Massachusetts State Police van parked on the street. He saw the Whale Center sign hanging above the door, and was surprised that it was an old house and not a commercial or academic-looking building.

"These are the people who are standing between me and a multi-billion-dollar gas deal?" he wondered in disbelief. He sat on a split rail fence and lit a cigarette as he stared at the Whale Center.

"Can I help you?" a deep voice behind him said.

Angus turned around quickly and was startled to see a very large policeman holding a sandwich in one hand and a Diet Coke in the other. In a glance, he noticed the name on the officer's badge, his rank, and the sidearm that he carried; a Glock 9mm, just like the one he had in his knapsack.

"No, I just wanted to visit and learn about whales, but I guess they're closed, right?"

"Right" Chief Souza said. "They'll probably be open again tomorrow. For now, this is a crime scene. Why don't you try one of the whale watch boats? My son's the captain of the Explorer. They have a four o'clock trip."

"Oh, right, well that's very helpful. Thanks. I'll look into that."

This was getting too close for Angus' liking. He quickly stood up and started walking back in the direction from which he came.

"Excuse me, sir?" Chief Souza called after him. "I think you dropped something."

Angus's blood ran cold as he turned to see the police chief holding the knife he'd just purchased. "Right, thanks."

"Where'd you get this?" Chief Souza asked.

"I just bought it at a store in town."

"The Surplus Store?"

"Yeah, that's it. It's just a souvenir."

"I see. Be careful with that, you could hurt yourself," the Chief said as he handed the knife back to Angus.

"I will, thank you." Angus turned again and walked briskly away, trying not to look any more suspicious than he felt he did now.

"Who was that?" State Trooper Stan Larchowski said to Chief Souza as he stepped out of the van.

"Some tourist, sounds English. Claimed that he came here to find out about whales, but he doesn't look like the crunchy type, not with the knife he's carrying. God, I wish they wouldn't sell those."

"Should we watch him?" Officer Larchowski asked.

"He hasn't done anything illegal. Besides, I got a good look at him. He shouldn't be too hard to find if we need to."

Angus could hear their conversation echo down the street.

"Damn" he said under his breath as he walked away from the officers. "Damn, damn, damn."

Chapter 19

"There's a few things I'd like to show you in here. Put these on." Trooper Larchowski handed Chief Souza a pair of latex gloves and shoe covers from a box on the front step. He had over twenty years of investigating homicides for the Massachusetts State Police. Chief Souza knew him both by name and reputation.

"All right, what'd you find?" the Chief said as he ducked under the yellow police tape and entered the Whale Center's first floor.

"Let's go upstairs, that seems to be where it all took place." The two men ascended the squeaky wooden staircase to the second floor.

"Here's what I think happened. The victim came in and surprised whoever was rifling through this office." Trooper Larchowski pointed to Linda Hanscomb's office door. "I don't think she ever made it to the top. Maybe she saw the person and turned around to run out, but they caught up with her on the stairs. See this damage to the plaster? We found hairs and some blood there that matches that of the deceased. She either tripped or was pushed down the stairs to this landing and her head was slammed into the wall."

"The autopsy said Dr. Hanscomb was strangled. Are you saying that she was killed by blunt force?"

"All I know for sure is that there are depressions in the plaster of the wall that contained her blood or hair. She was strangled, I don't dispute that, but she may have already been nearly dead by the time that happened. Then, we found more of her blood on the stairs and at the front door."

"So they just dragged her out the front door? And nobody saw anything? OK, then what?"

"Then, I don't know. The blood trail disappears on the street. I'm guessing that her body was put into a car and transported to the boat then dumped at sea."

"How about fingerprints?" Chief Souza asked hoping that some clue would at least point toward a particular person.

"We found over thirty different sets of fingerprints on the stair rails and the doors. This is a pretty busy place. You'll need to get fingerprints from everyone who works here so that we can go through and look for a match. We did find just two sets of prints on the stuff that was thrown around the office. One was from the deceased, but the other wasn't. I'm guessing that's your killer. I sent them out to be processed, but I haven't heard back yet."

"That's not much to go on, but it's a start, isn't it? All right, thanks. I'm heading back to my office to look over the autopsy reports. Let me know if anything else turns up."

"Sure thing, Chief."

Chief Souza walked out and ducked under the police tape. As he opened the door to his car, he realized that he was still wearing the booties and latex gloves.

He thought about his first murder investigation, the one that still haunted him. The "Lady in the Dunes" from 1974 who had never been identified or even reported missing. This case was clearly different. Linda Hanscomb was well known and well liked in town. Her death would not pass without notice, and the killer was likely still nearby, or so he hoped.

He removed the latex gloves and boot covers and threw them onto the passenger seat. He started the engine and slowly drove down the narrow street. Turning right, then right again, he was back on Shankpainter Road, and in less than five minutes, walked through the front door of the Provincetown Police Department Headquarters.

"Hey Chief," he heard Betsy Gilmore squawk from behind him as he entered the air conditioned lobby. "Do you have a second? I've got a couple of questions about the Linda Hanscomb case."

He just about snapped. "Betsy, I've got a lot of questions about this case, too. Until I've got them sorted out, I can't make any further comments to the media. Check with the front desk and they'll tell you when the next press conference is scheduled."

"Sure, Chief, I understand. Just one thing, since her hands and feet were bound with polyester rope like they use on the lobster boats, doesn't that mean her killer was probably a local guy?"

Chief Souza stopped dead in his tracks and turned to face Betsy. He could feel his blood pressure rising, and, from the look of fear on Betsy's face, he must have appeared as if he was ready to explode.

"How do you know about that?" he said gritting his teeth.

"I have sources."

"And you won't tell me who they are, will you?"

"I'm afraid not, Chief. Freedom of the press, you know how it is."

"Oh yeah, I know how it is." Chief Souza turned, entered his security code into a keypad next to the door, and stormed down the hall to his office.

"So, Chief, you think the killer's a local right?" Betsy hollered after him.

He heard her question, but he was too angry to respond. Someone was leaking sensitive information to the media which would inevitably tip off the suspect. In her quest to get a story, Betsy Gilmore was endangering this entire case.

Slamming his office door, he could still hear her question echoing in his head. "Dammit," he said aloud, "she's probably right."

He sat down behind his desk and picked up the receiver on the phone. His massive forefinger pressed the 5th speed dial number which connected him directly to the District Attorney's office in Barnstable.

"Mark Ryder" the voice on the line said.

"Mark, it's Bill Souza."

"Chief, how's the investigation coming?"

"It would be better if someone in your office wasn't leaking autopsy information directly to the media."

"Hold on a minute. What are you talking about? The pregnancy thing?"

"Yeah, that, and now Betsy Gilmore just informed me that the rope used to tie the hands and feet on the body is the same as what's used for lobster traps. I've barely read the entire autopsy report myself and some local hack reporter is practically quoting it to me. I don't know where she gets her information, but she's going to blow this entire case if the leaks don't stop."

"And you're assuming the leak is coming from my people? Think about it. There were over a hundred people on the boat when she was found, then the paramedics, the nurses at the hospital, and the coroner's office; they all saw the body, they all saw the rope. What are the odds that one of them knew something about lobstering? Pretty good, I would think. Look, I sympathize with you, and I promise that if find that one of my people is leaking to the press I'll come down on them like a ton of bricks, but a lot of people saw Linda Hanscomb's body."

"How about the pregnancy? You couldn't tell that by

looking."

"No, you couldn't, but there might have been other people who knew she was pregnant. What about her girlfriend who tried to kill herself?"

"As far as I know she didn't talk to any reporters before we took her in on the firearms charge. Look, all I'm saying is that we need to be careful. Betsy Gilmore right now seems to know more about this case than I do and I'm not happy about it. She's getting good information from someone very close to the case."

"I understand. Listen, Chief, not to change the subject but, do we know who the father is?"

"The father of Linda Hanscomb's baby? I've no idea."

"That's important to find out. Mary Ellen Johnson might be able to tell us something."

"I don't think she's going to talk to me right now. Remember, I broke three of her ribs this morning?"

"You also saved her life, don't forget that. I can go over to the hospital in a little while and try to persuade her to help us out."

"What do you mean persuade?"

"With prior felony convictions under her belt, she knows she's automatically facing jail time for illegal firearms possession. How about we cut her a deal that if she helps us investigate the murder, we'll drop the charges against her?"

"Okay by me, but only if we get full cooperation from her. I feel sorry for her. It seems like she was trying to start her life over after prison. She hasn't been any trouble at all since she's been in Provincetown."

"I agree with you. Let's give her a chance to do the right

thing."

"That sounds good to me, Mark. Call me once you talk to her."

"I will. Talk to you later."

When Chief Souza hung up the phone, he reflected on his years of experience with murders. Those who were closest to a murder victim could provide the best leads or were often the killers themselves. Now that the D.A. was off to talk to Mary Ellen Johnson, he needed to speak with the others who knew Linda best, Annie Macalister and Dr. Bruce Waters.

Chapter 20

"That's it Annie, you've got it, now cut the line!" Bruce shouted excitedly.

Annie reached out with a sharp serrated blade and quickly cut through the black polyethylene ropes that were wrapped around the whale's mouth. She was inches away from the enormous eye of the finback. By the look of the whale's eye, Annie swore it understood what she was trying to do.

"OK, just one more of these damn ropes. Stay calm now," Annie muttered to reassure both herself and the whale.

"You're doing great, Annie. Once you cut this one free, you'll release the pressure on the left blowhole. You'll have to pull the rope away from the infected area. That might make her a little jumpy."

"Jumpy?" She hated Bruce's euphemisms.

"It's kind of like pulling off a bandage that's stuck to a wound. She won't like it much, but once it's done she'll be able to breathe a lot better."

"OK, here we go." Annie cut the rope near where it hung into the water. She grabbed hold of the loose line and, with a snap, pulled it free from the whale's blowhole.

The whale immediately exhaled through the top of its head, spraying Annie with a fine mist that smelled like rotting flesh. She looked at her arms and saw droplets of blood splattered on her bare skin, like a Jackson Pollock painting. Gagging, she sat down on the wooden bench seat of the Zodiac.

"Welcome to the club!" Bruce said, laughing. "You've been baptized!"

"I think I'm going to be sick," Annie groaned.

"Well, don't take too long to catch your breath. There's still gear caught around the right fluke."

"OK, give me a minute." Annie fought the urge to vomit over the side of the boat. She didn't want to embarrass herself in front of Bruce and Juicy, plus she felt that it would be disrespectful to the whale.

Bruce maneuvered the small inflatable to the opposite side of the whale. Juicy followed them in the main rescue boat, to watch for their safety and to capture all of the proceedings on videotape. Tapes and DVDs of whale rescues were big sellers at the Whale Center Gift Shop.

"You ready, Annie?" Bruce yelled.

"Yeah, I'm fine. What do we need to do now?"

"We need to slow her down so that we can cut the gear off of that flipper." Bruce pointed to a trailing wake caused by ropes wrapped around the right pectoral fin. "If we're lucky, this will go quickly and she'll be on her way."

"And if we're not?" Annie asked.

"We can track her for days with the satellite buoy that we attached earlier. We'll just keep trying. Get the parachute ready."

Annie lifted the ball of rope and nylon fabric from the bow of the Zodiac and prepared to attach it to one of the ropes dragging from the whale's flipper. Grasping a boat hook in her other hand, she reached out and snagged a piece of rope from the water.

It's black poly rope, just like I've seen Shane using on his lobster traps, she thought. Why didn't he just spend the money and buy the new sinking line? The Whale Center even subsidized half the cost. I'll have to lean on him when I get back to shore.

"Come on Annie. Attach the chute before she tries to dive again," Bruce barked from the stern of the Zodiac.

Annie was startled back to the tasks at hand. "OK, it's on."

"Let it go!"

Annie splashed the parachute into the water. The effect on the whale's forward motion was immediate. In a response to danger, the finback tried to make a deep dive, but the large floats that had been attached made this impossible. Bruce sensed that the animal was getting anxious about not being able to move freely. He shifted the outboard motor into reverse and began to back away from the whale.

"Look out!" Juicy shouted to them from the rescue boat. Annie turned around just in time to see the massive tail fluke come completely out of the water and splash back down with tremendous force, just missing the side of the Zodiac by a few feet. She held on tight to the seat while the lightweight boat rolled up on it's side.

Annie thought for sure that they would capsize. Even though it was late August, the water temperature was only just above sixty degrees, not life-threatening cold, but uncomfortable none the less. When the boat came down without overturning, Annie heaved a sigh of relief.

"Whoa. That was close!" She said turning to Bruce, but he was not in the boat. "Bruce! Bruce!" Annie shouted as she scrambled to the stern.

"He's right there behind you!" Juicy yelled.

Annie saw him in the water, his life preserver keeping him afloat.

"Sonafabitch!" Bruce yelled while holding his right shoulder.

"Are you all right?" Annie and Juicy asked in chorus.

"I think I dislocated my shoulder. Oh, man, it hurts."

"Here, take my hand." Annie reached over the side of the inflatable to Bruce's good arm. He grabbed hold of her with his left arm, as his right dangled in the water. She pulled him towards the boat until he could hold onto the side by himself.

"Pull me up" Bruce groaned.

"I'll try. We've got to get you out of the water somehow."

"Damn right. It's freezing."

"Try to pull yourself up with your good arm, and I'll grab the back of your life vest and get the rest of you on board. On the count of three, ready? One, two, three!"

Bruce screamed in pain as Annie lifted with all of her 110 pounds of strength. She fell backwards on the seat as Bruce swung his legs into the Zodiac.

"Are you OK?" Annie asked.

"I think so, as long as it's not broken."

"You OK, mon?" Juicy said while he brought the rescue boat along side the Zodiac.

"Yeah, Juice, but I'm going to need your help."

"Whatever you need, mon."

"OK, first help me get on board." Bruce stood up and extended his left hand to Juicy. He winced in pain as he stepped up onto the deck of the rescue boat. "Help Annie aboard, then tie up the Zodiac."

Juicy turned to help Annie, but she was already pulling

herself up onto the deck with the bowline from the inflatable in her hand. She bent over and fastened the line around a deck cleat using figure 8 knots, just like Billy Sousa showed her on the Explorer.

"Juicy, I need you to pop my shoulder back into place."

"You're kidding, right mon? I'm no doctor."

"I'm not kidding. We're twenty-five miles out to sea. It will take hours to get back, then get to a hospital. It's got to be done, now."

"Mon, I don't know how to do that."

"I know how," Annie said.

"You do?" Bruce looked at her with a mix of puzzlement and relief.

"When I was hiking Mount Katadhin in Maine with some friends last year, one of them slipped off the Knife Edge trail and dislocated her shoulder when she hit a rock. There was nowhere to go, so I helped her put it back into the socket. It's going to hurt, though."

"It can't be much worse than it hurts now. Let's do it," Bruce said calmly.

"OK. Have a seat. Juicy, find some dry clothes and something we can use for a sling, like a towel or a T-shirt."

"Right." Juicy disappeared into the cuddy cabin.

"Annie, you've done a great job today, especially with everything else that's going on. Thanks."

"Thanks for believing in me." Annie wrapped one arm around his chest and held Bruce's limp arm in her other hand. With an upward, twisting motion, she repositioned the shoulder until she could both feel and hear the ball joint click into its socket.

131

Bruce screamed and started to shake. Annie wasn't sure if it was from the cold, wet clothing, or if he was going into shock from the pain. Either way, she knew from the first aid course she took in high school that he needed to get warm.

"Juicy, we need to get these wet clothes off him. You take his pants, I'll cut the shirt off. Bruce, how're you doing?"

"It actually feels better. I can take my own clothes off, just help me out of the life jacket."

Annie undid the three plastic buckles and slid the wet vest off of him.

Bruce looked around and said, "Hey, where's the whale?"

Annie had nearly forgotten about what led them there in the first place. "She's gone. But look, there's the parachute, and there's all the rope. Oh my God, she's free!"

Bruce slapped her on the back with his good arm, "You did it, Annie. You just saved a whale's life. It feels good, doesn't it?"

One hundred yards away from the boat, they saw the finback rise to the surface and exhale before diving deep and free for the first time in months.

Annie stared across the water and said in a whisper, "It does. It sure does."

Chapter 21

Angus checked his watch nervously. It was only 3:00 in the afternoon. He still had hours before he would meet with his accomplice. Still shaken from his close call with the local constabulary, Angus spent the rest of the afternoon in a small bar he'd found in the basement of a waterfront motel.

It was quiet when he first arrived. Angus was able to nurse a beer for nearly an hour in solitude while he collected his thoughts. Over the past half hour, a number of well tanned and muscular young men began to congregate around the bar and he noticed a DJ setting up his equipment in the corner. He could see that something was going to happen soon, and his beer glass was nearly empty. I'll hide here in the dark, he thought. Angus walked across the room to the bar and patiently waited until he caught the bartender's eye.

"Another Guinness," he said to the barman. As he waited for his refill, three bare-chested men sporting handlebar mustaches, leather riding chaps, and little else stepped up the bar beside him.

"Hi," one of them said to Angus.

"Hello," he replied curtly trying to neither make eye contact nor stare at the man's pierced nipples.

"First time, right?"

"I beg your pardon?"

"This is your first tea dance, isn't it? I can tell. You look nervous. I was nervous my first time, too."

"No, really, I just came in for a drink. It's pretty hot outside," Angus stammered. What the hell is taking that bartender so long to get one lousy beer? he thought as the DJ started playing "We Are A Family."

"Well, judging by the present company, I'd say it's pretty hot in here, too." The stranger smiled coyly.

Angus realized that he was being flirted with, something which had not happened to him in decades. He felt mildly flattered, but also annoyed at having drawn more attention to himself.

"Are you chatting me up?" Angus asked already knowing the answer.

"Chatting me up?" The stranger mocked his voice. "That's so cute. So, what are you, English?"

"No, I'm Scottish."

"Scottish, well, where's your kilt? I'm just kidding. But seriously, is it true that you don't wear anything under a kilt?"

"Yes," Angus answered through gritted teeth.

"How I love a man in a skirt! Or at least I'd like to!"

"Here you go, sorry about the wait; we had to change the keg." The bartender placed the beer in front of Angus. "That'll be $4.25." Angus handed him a five dollar bill.

"So, tell me Braveheart, are you here with anybody? Cause if you're not…" he ran his hand up Angus' thigh. Angus felt his blood pressure rising. He quickly brushed the man's hand away. "It's okay." The stranger persisted while lightly tracing his finger along Angus' muscular arm.

Angus responded in kind by placing his hand on the man's chest, and then firmly grabbed hold of the gold hoop protruding through the left nipple. He then proceeded to rotate it 360 degrees while pushing him to the floor. The man was in too much pain to speak.

"Now listen mate, I'm not interested in you or your friends.

I just want to enjoy my beer in peace. Understand?"

"Hey, what the hell are you doing? Leave him alone." The man's friends shouted.

Angus quickly assessed his situation. There were at least a dozen fit looking men staring at him with varying degrees of menace in their eyes. He was vastly outnumbered. This was not the way he envisioned his plans. He released his victim, put the beer down on the bar, and turned around to pick up his backpack.

He stood up in time to see the fist just before it made contact with his face, about an inch below his left eye. "You think you're cute? Huh? What's your problem?" Angus's suitor was back on his feet and ready to lay another blow on him.

Angus's head was still spinning from the punch. "I've got no problem with you. I just want to be left alone, that's all."

"Well, it's a little late for that now, isn't it?"

Angus felt powerful hands seize each of his arms as the man with the bruised nipple wound up for another punch. He hadn't been in a bar fight for a long time, but he remembered the rules clearly: There were none. A slight smile washed over Angus's face. The rush of adrenaline brought a flashback to the time when he left three Australian sailors with broken bones outside of a Bangkok massage parlor thirty years ago.

Angus's instincts took over. He smashed his foot down on the instep of the man to his right and heard a satisfying crunch of metatarsal bones snapping. The man immediately dropped to the floor screaming in pain. With his free hand, Angus retrieved the knife in his pocket, snapped it open, and , in an instant spun the man to his left around.

Angus was now standing behind him, twisting his wrist into an arm lock with one hand while holding the blade to the side of the surprised man's face. He slowly backed toward the door. Nobody in the bar moved, except the bartender who was dialing a phone.

"I'm going to walk out that door, and nobody's going to follow me. Understand? I don't want any more trouble."

Angus backed through the doorway, released his human shield, and ascended the steps up to the street level. He unlocked the blade and slipped the knife back into his pocket. He needed somewhere to go until he could move freely under the cover of darkness. Trying to walk up the street as inconspicuously as possible, Angus folded himself into a crowd of tourists and headed towards MacMillan Wharf.

Retracing his steps from earlier in the day, he reached the wharf in five minutes. As he walked along the pier, he saw a sign leaning against a small kiosk offering a four- hour sunset whale watch cruise. "What time does the next cruise leave?" he asked the attendant.

"Five minutes."

Angus checked his watch. It was 3:55 p.m. He could be on the boat until 8, well after the sun set. "How much?"

"Twenty-two dollars."

Angus pulled out his wallet and handed over the money.

"Here's your ticket. Better get going, they're ready to depart."

"Thanks." Angus took his ticket and clambered down the gangway. Anxiously, he waited in line as a deckhand ripped each ticket. He scanned the pier to see if any police or vigilantes had followed him. Seeing none, he stepped up onto the deck in time to hear a voice come over the loudspeaker. "Welcome aboard the Explorer, Provincetown's premiere whale watch and research vessel. Our Captain, Billy Souza, says that as soon as everyone's on board, we'll be underway for a memorable sunset cruise."

Chapter 22

District Attorney Mark Ryder was buzzed through the secure doors at Cape Cod Hospital's Psychiatric Facility. The low-slung building was separate from the main part of the Hospital, where those with a high risk of suicide were monitored under twenty-four hour care while also having their illnesses or injuries treated.

"I'm Mark Ryder and I'm here to see Mary Ellen Johnson," he said to Attendant Donna Gomes at the front desk.

"Oh, right. You called about an hour ago. Just sign in and we'll bring her to Room 3. You can wait for her there. It's the second door on the left." Donna pointed down the hall.

"Thanks." Mark walked down the hall to another secure door and waited for Donna to buzz him through. He entered the undecorated room through a shatter-resistant glass door and sat down at a round wooden table. After nearly ten minutes, Mary Ellen, wearing only a hospital gown and slippers, entered, escorted by a nurse.

He stood to greet her as she entered the room. "Hello, Ms. Johnson, I'm District Attorney Mark Ryder, please have a seat."

Mary Ellen averted his eyes as she shuffled in and sat on the wooden chair. Mark wondered if she had been sedated.

"I'll be right outside if you need me," the nurse said.

"So, how are you feeling?" Mary Ellen just sat in the chair, staring down at the table. "I understand you've been through a lot in the last twenty-four hours. Chief Souza showed me your criminal record, but he also said that you haven't been in any trouble since you moved to Provincetown, until this morning, that is. How long have you been living in P-Town?"

"About three years," Mary Ellen muttered. Mark was pleased that she talked.

"And before that, you were incarcerated in Florida, right?"

"Yeah. Look, I don't have to talk to you without a lawyer here."

"I understand. You're completely right; you don't have to talk to me. But I think you should."

"Why's that?"

"Because if you give us full cooperation in finding out who killed Linda Hanscomb, Chief Souza and I are willing to drop the firearms charges against you."

"So I don't go back to prison?"

"You don't go back to prison, but, we need you to cooperate with us 100%. If we find that you are withholding any information, we'll file the firearms charges, as well as obstruction of justice, and anything else that we can think of. Do you understand?"

Mary Ellen finally looked up and met Mark's gaze. "I understand. I'll tell you everything I know. Believe me, nobody wants to find who killed Linda and our baby more than I do."

"Good, so long as we understand each other. Let's start with Florida. You killed a man and served 10 years for manslaughter. Tell me what happened."

"I don't want to talk about Florida." Her head drooped again.

Mark slammed his briefcase shut and started to stand up. "That's what I thought. I'll see you in front of the judge in a few hours." He was playing hardball and both of them knew it.

"Wait. OK, I'll tell you what happened."

Mark sat back down in his chair.

"I did the best I could to raise my little brothers. I was barely eighteen when we had to move out of my aunt's house. It was fine at first, but I think we wore out our welcome. I got an apartment with the money I'd saved waiting tables, but it wasn't enough to buy food, clothes, and pay the utilities. I answered an ad for a bar that was looking for dancers. They were promising $500 a night. I was young, pretty and stupid, so I did it. After a few weeks, the owner, Jimmy, told me that I wasn't bringing in enough money, and he was going to fire me. I begged and pleaded, because I really needed the money. He said OK, but he wanted me to do him some favors."

"What kind of favors?"

"He was selling coke on the side. A lot of the girls were buying it. He asked me to let him keep a stash at my apartment. Jimmy said the cops were on to him, but if I let him keep it at my place, I could keep my job, and he'd give me an extra $50 a night."

"So you did it?"

"Yes, I did. I didn't know what else to do. After a while, I started using cocaine myself. Jimmy accused me of stealing from his stash, which I was. He threatened to kill me and my brothers if I didn't turn tricks for him. Nothing was ever good enough for him. He beat me almost every night, telling me that I didn't bring in enough money, or that I was stealing his coke. One night, I came home and I found Jimmy sitting in the living room with Wendell, my youngest brother. It was obvious that he had gotten Wendell high and he was trying to recruit him to sell drugs at his middle school. I freaked out. I'd bought a gun not long before to keep in my purse after I got beat up pretty bad by a john. I didn't even think twice. He'd already ruined my life and I wasn't going to let him ruin my brother's. I shot him three times in the chest. By the time the police got there, he was dead."

"You don't sound very remorseful."

"I'm not. I did the world a favor by getting rid of a piece of trash like Jimmy."

"Was it worth going to prison? That was ten years of your life taken away."

"You don't understand Mr. Ryder, those prison years were the ten best years of my life. I had a clean bed every night, food to eat, doctors if I needed them. I got sober, I got an education, I figured out who I really was. In some ways going to prison was the best thing that ever happened to me."

Mark nodded. He'd heard other people say the same thing before, but he could still never comprehend it fully.

"How about your brothers?"

"They're both fine. Wendell's a firefighter in Winston-Salem and Tony went to Morehouse on a football scholarship. He's practicing law now in D.C. They both learned from my example, what not to do." Mary Ellen almost smiled at the thought.

"So, how did you end up in Provincetown?"

"Same way a lot of people do. It's the end of the road, there isn't any further you can run. The day I got out of prison I headed north. The south is no place for a black lesbian with a degree in art history. I ended up in Boston and worked at a couple of galleries. I spent a weekend in P-Town and that was it. I went back to Boston, quit my job, packed my things, and never looked back. I had some help to get a business loan and I leased the gallery building on Commercial Street. I met Linda not long after that."

The D.A. paused to process her story, and decided to believe her before pressing further. "I have some questions about Linda."

"OK," she mumbled.

"Was she still married to Bruce Waters when you met her?"

"She was, but she wasn't happy. We were friends at first, but became more than that after a few months."

"How did Bruce take it?"

"He was furious, hurt, depressed. I felt bad for him, but you can't help who you fall in love with."

"Did he ever threaten Linda, or you?"

"No. I think they knew that they still needed to work together, so they tried to be friendly. Bruce doesn't like me much, I'm sure, but he's never threatened me."

"Is he the father of Linda's baby?" Mark was hoping to catch her off guard.

Mary Ellen looked shocked, and then laughed. "Bruce? No, Bruce and Linda tried to have kids when they were married, but it turns out he has a really low sperm count. We used to joke and call him O.B.B., One Ball Bruce. Linda and I went to a clinic up in Cambridge. We don't know who the donor was, probably some Harvard student."

"So, did Bruce even know that Linda was pregnant?"

Mary Ellen's eyes welled up with tears. "No, I don't think so. But she was going to tell him the night she was killed. She just never got the chance."

Or did she? Mark thought to himself.

Chapter 23

Annie was at the helm of the Whale Center rescue boat as they rounded the tip of Provincetown. She looked to her left and saw the old weather-beaten Coast Guard Station near Race Point Beach. This was nearly the exact spot where yesterday she and Juicy hauled Linda's body onto the deck of the Explorer.

She looked around the boat. Bruce sat next to her, holding his arm in the sling that Annie fashioned out of a T-shirt. Juicy leaned against the stern, staring out at the water. She wondered if he, too, was thinking about what happened. For a moment, their eyes met. From the sad look he gave, she knew instantly that he was. All three were silent as the boat skipped over the waves.

When they were off shore of Herring Cove Beach, the large white hull of the Explorer came into view about a mile away. Annie knew that Captain Billy always kept his VHF radio on channel 11, so she made sure that her's was on the same frequency.

"Whale Rescue One to Whale Watch Vessel Explorer. Do you copy?" Annie had spent a lot of time on the bridge next to Billy and she learned the nautical protocol.

"This is Explorer. That you Annie?" She heard Billy's voice over the speaker.

"Yeah, Billy, we're on our way back in."

"Already? How'd you do?"

"It went pretty quickly. We freed her in about three hours."

"Nice job guys. Come up alongside us, I'll have the passengers give you a cheer."

"OK." Annie said with a nervous laugh.

Annie backed the throttle down as she approached the Explorer. She enjoyed the power and agility of the rescue boat and appreciated Bruce's reluctance to give up the controls. She could hear the voice of Joyce Eldredge, a Whale Center volunteer in her late seventies using the public address system on the Explorer.

"Ladies and gentlemen, here are some real heroes. This is the whale entanglement rescue team from the Provincetown Whale Center. They just helped free a finback whale that was entangled in lobster gear off Truro. Let's show them our appreciation and give them a round of applause."

Annie looked up at the open top deck and saw hundreds of people waving, clapping, and recording them on video. Annie and Juicy waved back to the crowd while Bruce smiled and nodded.

Angus Black was staring right down at her. Annie squinted, recognized him, and waved to him.

"Hi, Tom! Hey, Bruce, look, that's the guy who helped me earlier today." Annie pointed directly at Angus. "Tom Lawrence, what a charmer. Hi, Tom, enjoy the trip! Huh, why isn't he waving?"

"That's enough of the limelight, let's get back to the dock. Go ahead and open her up, Annie."

"You got it!" she replied with a big grin on her face. She pushed the twin throttles slowly forward and lowered the trim tabs to keep the nose of the boat level. The acceleration was immediate. She and Bruce were nearly pinned to their seats while Juicy braced himself against the aluminum frame of the boat's canopy.

Annie looked down at the GPS which also registered the forward speed of the boat. They were going fifty-eight miles per hour. She thought that on a weekend day in July, there wasn't a single car on Cape Cod going that fast.

"Why would the Coast Guard ever give up a boat like this?" She shouted into Bruce's ear.

"Because the smugglers have even faster ones."

Annie just shook her head in disbelief as the wind whipped past her. Their burst of speed was short-lived, as they reached the Long Point Lighthouse in less than two minutes. She slowed the boat to a more respectable twenty miles per hour as they entered the outer part of Provincetown Harbor. Once past the breakwater, she backed the throttle to idle speed as they approached the dock they shared with the Explorer.

"You want to dock it, Annie?" Bruce asked.

"You trust me?"

"So far so good. Just ease it right in."

Juicy had already dropped the white rubber bumpers over the side so that the boat wouldn't rub against the dock. Annie turned the wheel and let the boat drift sideways to the pier.

"Put it in reverse and swing your ass end around," Bruce said matter of factly.

"Excuse me?"

He realized he was sounding a little too local. "Sorry, bring the stern around."

"Gotcha."

Annie inched the boat into position and felt a soft bump when it contacted the floating dock.

"Nice job." Bruce said. "You too, Juicy. Good work today, both of you. Let's get everything tied up and I'll buy you both dinner."

"Sounds good, mon! Where we eatin'?" Juicy asked as he secured the dock lines.

"How about burgers and beer at the Post Office? What do you say, Annie?"

"Fine, I haven't eaten since this morning. I'm starving."

Annie and Juicy finished putting everything away on the boat while Bruce waited for the handful of painkillers he took to kick in. Once everything was stowed away, Annie locked the cabin door and put the keys in her shorts pocket. She made a mental note to hang them up in the key locker back at the center.

The three walked down MacMillan Wharf and turned left onto Commercial Street. They walked into the Post Office Café and sat at a table next to the window. This was a prime spot for people-watching which was, by far, Annie's favorite pastime in Provincetown. It was from this very spot that she once witnessed a drag queen on roller skates, dressed as Scarlet O'Hara, glide by while reciting: "with God as my witness, I'll never go hungry again!" The image was indelibly etched into Annie's mind.

When a waiter approached their table, Annie immediately recognized him. She was one of Brad's regular customers.

"Hi, Annie. Jeez, what happened to you? You look like hell."

Annie looked down at her shirt and realized it was spattered with blood from the whale. She hadn't seen herself in the mirror since 6:00 a.m., and was suddenly feeling very self conscious.

"Annie freed a whale today, but it got a little messy," Bruce said with pride.

Brad was duly impressed. "No kidding! I feel like such a slacker. I slept till noon, then came to work. Saving whales, that's so awesome."

"Thanks," Annie said sheepishly.

"So, can I get you three some drinks to celebrate?"

Bruce ordered a Sam Adams and Annie had the same. Juicy was pleased to see that they carried Red Stripe, his native beer from Jamaica. All three ordered cheeseburgers with French fries. They quietly stared out the window for a few minutes while they waited for the cold beer to arrive.

Annie learned in her first few days in Provincetown that the front table at the Post Office Café was one of the best seats in town. Behind their heads was a row of old post office boxes next to the bar. Looking out the window was like watching a microcosm of the entire world pass by. Annie enjoyed the constant parade, there were all sorts of couples strolling arm in arm, guys riding bicycles with parrots on their shoulders, people walking dogs with matching leather collars. She made a point to stop in at least every other day for a drink or meal.

When the beers arrived, Bruce offered a toast to Annie. They clinked bottles and drank in the hoppy coldness with gusto. In their efforts this afternoon, none of them had taken time to eat or drink anything.

Bruce thoughtfully peeled the label off his beer bottle. Finally, he turned to Annie.

"Do you think Mary Ellen killed Linda?"

"I don't know. I've asked myself that a hundred times today."

"She certainly was acting guilty this morning. Do you think she really would have killed herself?"

"That's what the cop said that I talked to this afternoon. That reminds me, I need to call the chief, he wants to talk to me."

"About what?" Bruce sounded nervous.

"About Mary Ellen, I guess. I don't really know for sure."

"Did you know she was pregnant?"

"Who? Mary Ellen?"

"No, Linda. I didn't know either. I heard it on the news conference this morning."

"Oh, my God. I had no idea. Who's the father?"

"I don't know. They asked me to be a donor about six months ago, but I said no way. They must have gone to a clinic or something."

"Now there's two murders aren't there? Linda and the baby," Juicy said sadly.

Brad came back with a tray full of cheeseburgers and fries. Despite their gloomy mood, all three of them were starving and began to eat immediately.

Bruce continued, "I just hope they find whoever did this soon. I'll tell you guys something that I haven't told anyone else, I don't think it was Linda they were after, but her research."

"Her research?" Annie sounded alarmed.

"The report that she was going to present to the EPA in a few weeks would have put the entire Gulf of Maine off limits to oil and gas exploration, or so we hoped. She established that the entire ecosystem was critical habitat for right whales. The increase in ship traffic alone is enough to wipe out the species. We had ten whales killed by ship collisions last year. That's over three percent of the species killed in one year. The biggest threat comes from the exploration. The oil companies use low frequency sonar to determine where to drill. These same frequencies disorient the whales, and some studies the Navy did showed that they caused them to beach themselves."

"I know all about this," said Annie. "I've been working to help Linda compile the research for her report."

"That's good because it all has to be done again. The hearings in Washington won't be postponed. We need to sort it all out and write a new report. Without Linda's testimony, the only ones to speak about oil drilling in the Gulf of Maine will be the oil companies. Whoever trashed her office smashed her laptop. She was very careful not to leave paper copies of the report lying around, so the only copy is in a secure file on her hard drive which is now dead."

Annie looked across the beer bottles at Bruce, then Juicy, then back to Bruce. In a low whisper she said, "That wasn't the only copy."

"What? Are you sure?" Bruce's hushed voice matched Annie's.

"Yes. She kept a draft copy on her computer at home, too."

"Does anyone else know about this?"

"Mary Ellen must know about it. Sometimes Linda and I would go to her house to work on it there. Mary Ellen's in jail and I'm sure the house is all locked up. I'll talk to the chief and see if he can let me in their house to get the report."

Lurking just outside the window, but out of Annie's view, Linda's murderer was listening intently to their entire conversation. He knew that the report was the bargaining chip he would need later that night and Annie would lead him right to it.

Chapter 24

The ringing phone on his desk startled Chief Souza as he combed through the details of Linda Hanscomb's autopsy report.

"Chief Souza," he answered gruffly.

"Hi Bill, it's Mark Ryder. I've been talking to Mary Ellen Johnson, she says she'll cooperate with the investigation."

"That's good news. Did you get anything out of her?"

"A little. She said that Bruce Waters isn't the baby's father. Linda went to a clinic in Boston and had an anonymous donor. She was on her way to tell him the night she was killed."

"Interesting. There's something about that guy that doesn't feel right."

"You've talked to him?"

"Yeah, last night I stopped by the Whale Center to look for some leads. I bumped into him. It was pretty late. He was cooperative, but I get the feeling he's hiding something. After we talked, I saw him go straight back to his house across the street. Not a minute later he was on the phone to someone and watching me from his window."

"Does he have access to a boat?"

Chief Souza could tell where the DA was going with this theory. He was heading in the same direction himself. "Sure. He has that old Coast Guard speedboat and a couple of Zodiacs."

"Well, let's see, ex-wife leaves him for a woman, then tells him she's pregnant. Guy goes into a rage, since he wasn't able to have kids with her himself, slams her head into the wall and strangles her, then dumps the body out at sea. You've got both motive and opportunity."

"Who told you that he couldn't have kids with her?"

"Mary Ellen. Said the guy was basically shooting blanks. I think you've got yourself a suspect there, Chief."

"Maybe so. I definitely want to talk to him. What's Mary Ellen's status?"

"She'll be OK. Two broken ribs, but it could have been worse."

"Good. Do you think she's a hazard to herself?"

"I think she's more of a hazard to whoever killed her girlfriend. She told me about what happened in Florida. She killed a man in cold blood to protect her family, with no regrets. I could only imagine what her revenge fantasies must be like. The hospital wants to keep her at the Psych Center for forty-eight hours to evaluate if she's a further danger. After that, who knows? They'll either release her or ship her up to the psychiatric hospital in Brockton for a couple of weeks. Either way, she's not going anywhere until at least Monday morning."

"All right, thanks for everything. I feel like we're starting to get somewhere. I'll talk to you later."

"OK, Chief."

As he hung up the phone, Dispatcher Carla Thompson knocked on the Chief's door.

"Come in. Hi, Carla."

"Hi, Chief. FYI, about thirty minutes ago there was a fight at the Below Decks lounge. Some guy pulled a knife and held it against another patron's neck. He took on three big men and left them all on the floor. No serious injuries, though one guy had a broken foot."

Chief Souza immediately had a hunch. "Was he English?"

Carla looked impressed. "Actually, the witnesses said he was Scottish, how'd you know?"

"I saw that guy earlier today, with his knife. He was hanging around the Whale Center watching the State Troopers collect evidence. We've got to find him, ASAP."

"Right, we've got a good description, so I'll let all patrols know who we're looking for."

"Tell everybody to be very careful. This guy's armed and dangerous. If he took on three men by himself, he's probably got some kind of military or martial arts training. If anyone spots him, they're not to engage without backup. Is that clear?"

"Roger that, Chief. I'll put out an APB right now."

"Thanks, Carla."

Chief Souza closed his eyes and breathed out a heavy sigh as soon as she shut his office door. Half of his summertime police force were college students with little training. They were fine for traffic duties and giving tourists directions, but the idea of one of them trying to subdue an armed suspect with hand-to-hand combat experience made him shudder. I need to find this guy myself, he thought, if this damn phone would ever stop ringing.

"Chief Souza."

"Hi, Chief, It's Annie Macalister."

"Annie, I'm glad you called. I've wanted to talk to you."

"Me, too. About this morning, I thought Mary Ellen killed herself, but I heard that you shot her with a beanbag or something? Is she hurt?"

"You did a great job this morning, Annie. Thanks to you, she'll be fine. I just spoke with someone who talked to her at Cape Cod Hospital."

"She's not a suspect in Linda's murder, is she?"

"I can't say that anyone is not a suspect right now. We just don't know enough about what happened yet, but there are some other leads that we're investigating."

"Chief, I really want to talk to you about Linda's research."

"Her research? Wait a minute, I hear a lot of noise on your end of the phone. Where are you?"

"I'm at the Post Office Café. My cell phone battery went dead this morning when I was talking to Mary Ellen. A friend of mine who's a waiter here is letting me use his phone. Hold on, let me step outside. Is that better?"

"Yes, much better. What about Linda's research?"

"Well, all summer I was her research assistant. We were compiling this big report for the EPA to put the entire Gulf of Maine off limits to oil drilling. It's possible that whoever killed Linda was trying to stop that report from becoming public."

"That would explain why they trashed her office and smashed the computer. So, you know everything that's in that report right?"

"Yeah, Linda and I spent all summer working on it."

Chief Souza felt another hunch coming on, "By any chance have you met a guy with a Scottish accent in the past few days? Somewhere between 50 and 60 years old?"

Annie was stunned. "You mean Tom? The guy who helped me when I fell this afternoon? What about him?"

Chief Souza pulled a silver Cross pen from his pocket and started to make notes on a pad of paper in front of him. "What did you say his name was?"

"Tom Lawrence."

"I think he might know something about Linda's murder. Do you have any idea where he is right now?"

"Are you kidding? He's on the Explorer. I just saw him less than an hour ago. He seemed so nice to me. He couldn't have killed Linda, anyway he said that he just came into Provincetown on this morning's ferry."

"I don't know if he killed Linda or not, but he's very dangerous. He assaulted three guys in a bar about an hour ago. The good thing is, we know where he is, and he can't get away. I'll call Billy on the Explorer right now, and we can have officers arrest him when they return. I think you're right, Annie, someone might be after that report."

"Do you think I'm in danger from Tom?" Annie said nervously.

"Tom Lawrence is a danger to everyone until we bring him in which we'll do soon. Will you help us identify him when the Explorer comes in?"

"Sure. Are you going to have them come back early?"

"No. I don't want to raise any suspicions. Just meet me at the dock around 7:30. Until then, just lay low. Anyway, I thought you were with Shane all day?"

"I was this morning, but after the whole Mary Ellen thing I came back to town. He went back out to pull lobster traps, then I ended up on a whale rescue with Bruce and Juicy."

Chief Souza paused. "Are you with Bruce Waters now, at

the Post Office Café?"

"Yes, we came back about half an hour ago. We're having something to eat."

"Do me a favor, Annie. Keep him there a little while longer. I'm on my way downtown, and I'd like to talk to you together."

Annie thought this was a little weird. "Um, OK. Hold on, I'm looking inside. I don't see him. He must have gone to the men's room or something."

"I'm on my way." He hung up the phone and quickly left his office to avoid answering another call.

On his way out the door, he poked his head into the dispatch room and said, "Carla, put out an APB for Bruce Waters. He was just seen at the Post Office Café. Tell the patrols that if he doesn't come in voluntarily for questioning, arrest him."

"Roger that, Chief."

Chapter 25

Angus stood at the rail of the Explorer with a crowd of tourists, enjoying the whale watch cruise. Where the other passengers saw whales feeding at the surface, Angus envisioned drilling platforms extracting millions of cubic feet of natural gas. With the demand rising throughout the US, and the cost of Middle Eastern oil skyrocketing, he knew that this deal would be worth billions to Scotia Gas. There was no way he could let the Whale Center's report reach the EPA in Washington.

He decided to keep his sunglasses on after seeing his black eye in the men's room mirror. Knowing that Annie Macalister spotted him on the boat made him uncomfortable, but he'd decided that he posed far greater threat to her than she did to him.

He felt the cell phone in his pocket vibrate. It was an odd sensation that took him a moment to recognize. He walked away from the crowd at the railing so that no one would overhear his conversation.

"Hello?"

"Mr. Black?" a gruff sounding voice croaked.

"Yes, is that you?"

"Yeah. Listen, I just overhead a conversation between the director of the Whale Center and some girl. She knows all about the report. She says there's another copy."

"Where?"

"Back at the house where Hanscomb lived with her girlfriend. It's on her computer."

"We have to get to it before anyone else does. Tell me

about the girl. Who is she?"

"Her name is Annie. She's young, still in college."

"I know her. We've got to get rid of her and the report."

"You mean kill her? Look, Mr. Black, you asked me to get you the report, not go on a killing spree. The first one was an accident. You want this one done, I want twenty five thousand."

"Our initial agreement was five thousand for the report. Since you bollixed that one up, this has become much more complicated. Bring the girl with you when we meet tonight and I'll pay you ten thousand cash. You don't have to get any more blood on your hands, I'll take care of her myself."

"How am I supposed to get her there?"

Angus gritted his teeth and raised his voice. "Listen, mate, my patience with you is running out. Have her there tonight or I'll put a bullet in the back of your head. Do you understand?"

"Yes, I understand."

Angus hung up in disgust. He knew that in all likelihood he would have to kill both of them. There was simply too much at stake.

"Everything OK here, sir?"

Angus nearly jumped out of his skin. He looked around and saw no one. Then he looked up and saw a large man wearing a light blue shirt with a captain's insignia on the lapel staring down at him from the stairway to the bridge. He tried to compose himself.

"Yes. Everything is fine thanks, just some bad news, that's all."

"I heard some yelling, and I wanted make sure everybody was all right," Captain Billy Souza said while sizing up the man his father had just described to him as the primary suspect in Linda Hanscomb's murder.

"Oh, yes, fine. Thanks for your concern."

"Well, if you want to see some whales, there's three finbacks feeding over there. You can see them just fine from the stern." Billy pointed to the stern.

"Sure, right. Well, thanks."

"You have a nice day, sir."

Billy Souza turned and ascended the metal stairs that led back to the bridge. "That's him," he said to his first mate Jack Taylor.

"So, what do we do?" Jack asked.

"I don't know. I'm going to call the chief back." Billy pressed the speed dial number for his father's cell phone.

"Chief Souza."

"Dad, it's Billy. I just saw the guy you described. It's definitely him. Looks like he's got quite a shiner, too. He's trying to cover it with sunglasses."

"What's he doing?"

"He was just on the phone with someone. Sounded pretty angry, too. I couldn't hear the whole conversation but I think he was threatening to shoot someone. What should I do?"

"Nothing. I don't want you to do anything that will arouse his suspicions. We don't really know who this guy is yet, or what he's up to, but he's armed with at least a knife and he isn't afraid to pull it out in public."

"Great. So I've got an armed suspect on board my ship, and

there's nothing I can do about it?"

"Look, Billy, just bring the boat in at the regular time, and I'll have my officers in street clothes to pick him up. Could you hear anything else he said?"

"He said something about bringing her with him when they meet. But I have no idea who he's talking about."

Chief Souza paused. "Annie," he said with a sigh.

"What's Annie got to do with this?" Billy was clearly concerned.

"I'm still not sure, but she thinks this has something to do with Linda Hanscomb's research. I'm starting to agree. She knows the contents of the report, and someone wants it stopped."

"I'm not following you, Dad. Linda was killed because of research about what whales eat and now the same guys are after Annie? There's got to be more to the story than this."

"I know, but that's all I've got for now. Look, I have to go. Keep an eye on that guy. We'll be waiting for him when you get back."

"Roger that. Be careful, Dad."

"You too, Billy."

Chief Souza punched the off button on his cell phone and parked his cruiser in the small plaza near the end of MacMillan Wharf. He turned and walked the 150 feet to the Post Office Café where he saw Annie and Juicy sitting at the front table looking nervous.

"Hi, Annie, Juicy. Where's Bruce?"

"I don't know," Annie replied. "I stepped outside to call you, and Juicy said he excused himself to go the men's room."

"But he's not in there. I checked." Juicy finished her sentence.

Annie was confused about the entire situation. "Chief, what's going on? Is Bruce a suspect too?"

"I just want to ask him a few questions, but his disappearing like this does raise some concern. I need to establish if he saw Linda the night she was killed."

"No, I didn't," Bruce said tersely from behind them.

Annie shot him an angry look. "Bruce, where did you go? What's going on?"

"I just went to my car to find a better sling for my arm." He motioned to the towel that he had tied around his shoulder.

"What happened to your arm?" Chief Souza inquired.

"I dislocated it. The whale flipped me out of the boat, and as I went over I smacked into the outboard motor. Annie here did a good job of popping it back in place, but I'll need a few more beers before the pain goes away." He sat down in his chair and took another sip from his bottle.

Chief Souza wanted to get back to business. "So, you said that you didn't see Linda Thursday night."

"No, the last time I saw her she was working in her office on the EPA report. I had to leave early to go to a fundraising dinner at Napi's with the board of directors."

"What time did the dinner finish?"

"Around eight, but some of us stayed for drinks until nearly midnight. I went home after that."

"You live right across the street from the Whale Center, did you see or hear anything when you got home?"

"No. It looked like all the lights were turned off, so I just went to bed."

"You didn't check to see if the door was locked or anything?"

"No, why should I? Everybody there knows to lock up if they're the last ones out of the building."

"And everybody remembers?"

"Pretty much. Don't you think so?" He glanced at Annie and Juicy. Both nodded.

"So, if the door was locked, how did someone get in? There was no sign of forced entry, no broken windows, no pry marks on the door."

"I don't know. It's possible that Linda was there working. She sometimes worked late at night. Maybe the door was open and the guy walked right in."

"Why would someone want to steal her research?"

"Why? Simple, money. In all likelihood there's as much oil and natural gas out there as in all of Texas. If the EPA allows drilling, whichever oil company gets the contract will make billions. People don't care much about what happens offshore if they can't see it. That's why this report is so important. The public has to be made aware of what's out there and what's at stake. If you want to find out who killed Linda, you need to find out who has the most to lose in this deal."

Chief Souza thought about this for a moment. He reconsidered his initial decision to arrest Bruce. "That's what I intend to do. But I'll need your help. Will you come back to the station with me and answer some questions about Linda and this report? I'd like to record it so that we don't miss any details."

"Sure, Chief. Whatever it takes, I've got nothing to hide."

Chief Souza helped him to his feet and led him out the door. "I hope you're right."

Annie and Juicy sat quietly as they watched Chief Souza walk Bruce back to the police car. His alibi made sense to her, but it was obvious that Bruce was being treated as a suspect.

"Juicy, I've got an idea. We need to get into Mary Ellen's house and make copies of that report. If we can get it out to the media now, whoever is trying to stop it will be too late."

"And they won't be after you or anyone else, right?"

"Hopefully. I've got to go back to my apartment and change my clothes. Can you meet me at Mary Ellen's in half an hour?"

"Sure, mon, but what do you want me to do?"

"Help me get in, and be a lookout."

"Yah, OK, but we need to be careful. I got a feelin' there's some bad folks around. The sooner the police catch that Tom guy the better."

"That's why we need to do it now before he gets back. OK, I'll meet you at the Dharma Gallery at six."

"You want me to come with you now?"

Annie stood to leave. "No, I'll be all right. I just want to shower and change out of these clothes. Hey, wait a minute. Bruce left without paying."

"It's okay Annie, I got it." Juicy pulled a surprisingly large wad of cash out of his pocket and peeled off two twenty dollar bills.

"Whoa, Juice, where'd you get that kind of money?"

161

"Billy pays me in cash. I don't have a bank account here, so I just keep it with me."

Annie shrugged her shoulders. She'd heard that Juicy always had more money than a deck hand would make. Rumor had it that he was supplying designer drugs to tourists, but she'd never believed it, until now. She and Juicy walked out the door and into the late afternoon sunshine. Squinting, Annie said "Thanks for paying, see you in half an hour."

<u>Chapter 26</u>

Annie walked up the wooden steps to her second-story apartment just off Commercial Street. The entrance to it was down a narrow side alley between two buildings. She turned the key in the lock and pushed, but the humidity had caused the wood to swell, making the door tight. She leaned her shoulder into it and the door opened. Just out of the corner of her eye she thought she saw someone else coming down the alley, but when she turned her head to look, no one was there.

Once inside the shoebox of an apartment, Annie closed the door and locked the deadbolt. She immediately plugged her cell phone into its charger, then she checked her answering machine which was blinking with four messages.

The first was from her mother. "Annie, I heard about the murder of the scientist at that place you work. It's just terrible. I hope everything's ok. Call me when you get this. Love ya, bye." Beep.

"Hey babe, it's Shane. It's like, four o'clock. Sorry about earlier. I was stressed about getting the traps done. I'm back at my place now. I tried you on your cell, but I remembered it's dead. Give me a call when you get in, maybe we can go out tonight. There's a good reggae band playing at the Beachcomber in Wellfleet. OK, talk to you later." Beep.

"Idiot," she muttered. "My life's in danger, I'm about to break into someone's house, and he wants to go out drinking."

"Hi, it's Mom again. I didn't hear back from you, I'm getting worried. Please call me when you get in. I love you. Bye." Beep.

"Hey babe, me again. I called Billy, and he told me you were out on a whale rescue. That's cool. I bet you're pretty tired. Why don't you get some sleep and I'll see you tomorrow. I'll come over in the morning." Beep.

"You clueless moron!" she shouted at the machine. Annie pressed the delete button with vengeance. While she did, the phone rang. If it was Shane again, she was going to let him have it for being so, well, Shane.

"Hello?" She barked into the receiver.

"Annie, it's Mary Ellen. Are you OK?"

"Oh, my God, Mary Ellen. Yes, yes, I'm OK. How are you?"

"I'm pretty sore, but other than that I'm all right. I didn't know what I was doing this morning. It was like I stepped out of my own body."

"I thought something horrible happened. It's so good to hear your voice."

"Thanks Annie, that's sweet. I'm wondering if you could do me a favor."

"Sure, anything you need."

"Could you go over to my house and feed my kitty Ray Charles? There's a key hidden inside a rock by the bird feeder."

Annie couldn't believe the timing. "Actually, Mary Ellen, I was hoping I could go over to your place. Linda kept a copy of her environmental impact report on the gas drilling on her home computer; I need to get a copy of it as soon as possible."

"Why? Can't that wait?"

"I don't think it can. Chief Souza thinks that someone might have been after that report when Linda was killed. There's a creepy guy in town named Tom that might be connected to all of this. I'm the only one who knows what's in that report, and the only copy is on the computer at your house. The sooner the report is made public, the better."

"Annie, do whatever you need to do to keep yourself safe. I don't want Linda's death to be in vain, so get that report. But be careful, that Tom guy sounds dangerous."

"That's what the Chief says, too. Don't worry, we'll get him, and the report too."

"Thanks Annie. Good luck. Oh, Ray Charles gets one can in the morning and one at night. Just make sure he has plenty of dry food and water, too."

Annie laughed. "If he doesn't, he's likely to eat me!" She'd never seen a cat as large as Ray Charles. "Don't worry. Everything will be fine. I'll call you tomorrow. You can get calls at the hospital, can't you?"

"Yeah, sure. I'll talk to you tomorrow. Thanks for everything. You're a good friend. Bye-bye."

"Bye Mary Ellen."

She immediately stepped into the bathroom and turned on the shower. While she waited for the hot water to come, she stripped off her foul smelling clothes, dumped them in the trash and stepped into the steaming shower. She felt the grime of the day start to wash off. She watched as the water at her feet changed colors from pink to brown and finally become clear. She would have liked to linger there, but she knew she had to meet Juicy.

She stepped out of the shower and wrapped herself in a towel. When she opened the bathroom door, she let out a scream as she saw a large man's silhouette peering through the front door window.

"Who are you!" she shouted. "Get out of here!"

The shadowy voyeur retreated hastily down the steps. Annie heard the footsteps fade as he ran up the alley.

She quickly double-checked the lock to make sure it was bolted, then went into her bedroom to dress. "Who was that?" she wondered aloud. "God, Annie, what have you gotten yourself into?" She put on a clean T-shirt and transferred the contents of her shorts pockets into a pair of jeans. She unplugged the cell phone which was just barely charged, and slipped it into her back pocket.

The little voice inside Annie's head, which she usually attributed to her grandmother, told her to be extra cautious. She rummaged through her purse for the can of pepper spray that her father had given her as a going away present in May. At the time, Annie thought he was greatly overestimating the dangers she might encounter in Provincetown, but now she was thankful for his foresight.

She opened the door slowly and looked around to see if there was anyone hiding in the alley. When she saw that it was clear, she slipped the small canister into her pocket and locked the door behind her. She moved as quickly as she could down the stairs and through the alley, feeling a little safer once she was in public view on Commercial Street.

Annie picked her way through the Saturday evening madness of Commercial Street. She'd forgotten that it was Fourth of July weekend, a time when just about anything could happen with tens of thousands of tourists in the streets.

Every few hundred feet, Annie looked over her shoulder to see if she was being followed, but with all of the people milling about it was impossible to tell. By the time she reached the East End Gallery district, the crowds had thinned out considerably. She saw the hand-carved, lotus shaped sign at the Dharma Gallery and her heart beat faster. Juicy was nowhere in sight.

She decided it would be safer for her to wait inside than out on the street, so she looked around the base of the bird feeder by the side door and found the hollowed rock containing the house key.

Annie opened the door and was greeted by the enormous black bulk of Ray Charles purring at her feet. She quickly closed the door behind her and locked it.

"Hi, Ray," she groaned as she picked him up. "Good kitty. Let me get you some food." Annie hurriedly fed Ray and gave him fresh water, then went into the home office that Linda shared with Mary Ellen. There were pictures all around of the two of them with their friends. Annie had seen them before, but never paid much attention to the vacation photos of San Francisco, New York, London, and a Caribbean cruise that Linda and Mary Ellen went on last winter. Now, the arrangements of pictures seemed more like a shrine to Linda's memory.

Annie suppressed the lump in her throat and sat down at the computer. She turned it on and waited while it warmed up. Ray Charles, who was starved for affection, climbed up into her lap, kneading her denim jeans with his giant double paws.

"Ouch! That's enough, Ray," she said as his claw dug into her leg.

She clicked on "Documents", and saw a list of many different folders. Finally, she found the Whale Center folder and tried to open it. Annie hadn't accounted for it being password protected.

Uh-oh, she thought, what could it be? Looking down at the pile of black fur curled up on her lap, she tried the obvious and typed in Ray Charles. She once heard that using a pet's name for a password was a bad idea because it could be so easily guessed. Apparently, Linda had heard this, too.

Annie typed in password after password, trying to think like Linda with no luck. Her head throbbed from the stress. "Where is

Juicy?" she said to Ray Charles.

A thought occurred to Annie to do a Google search for Thomas Lawrence. She spelled out the name and hit enter, and was surprised at how many hits she had for Lawrence of Arabia. No luck there either, she thought. Annie made a mental note to come back to this later.

She looked at the clock and saw that it was nearly seven. She needed to get down to MacMillan Wharf to help identify Tom Lawrence when the Explorer came in.

"OK, Ray, I'll be back later." Annie looked out the window on the side street to see if there was anyone watching her. Satisfied that she wasn't being followed, she opened the door wide enough to slip outside and pull it shut behind her. She checked to make sure that it was locked and then placed the key back under the rock. After one final glance around, she made her way through the crowds on Commercial Street to MacMillan Wharf.

Once he could see that Annie had left, the shadowy stranger watching her stepped out of the bushes of the house next door, and retrieved the key from its hiding place. He calmly let himself in, shut the door, and sat down at the computer.

Chapter 27

Angus knew that Annie had spotted him on the whale watch boat. He assumed that she didn't know his real identity, or the true reason for his visit to Provincetown, but even so, she was able to pick him out of a crowd, and that was a problem.

Since the exchange with the captain, Angus suspected that a crew member was watching him. Maybe I'm being paranoid, he thought for a moment, but experience had taught him better. Angus watched a deck hand change the garbage can liner for the third time in half an hour. Each time, he glanced at Angus as he took the near empty bag away.

As the Explorer approached the inner harbor of Provincetown, Angus stepped onto the deck and noticed a fellow passenger with a pair of binoculars hanging around his neck.

"Mind if I borrow those for a moment?"

"What? Oh, these? Yeah, sure, here you go."

"Thanks." Angus scanned the crowd of people waiting on the dock. It was difficult to see clearly since the sun had set, but in the twilight he could see Annie standing next to the police chief.

"Are you looking for someone?" the stranger asked.

"Yes, I'm supposed to meet someone for dinner. They're there. Thanks." He handed the binoculars back.

"No problem."

Actually, big problem, Angus thought. Big, stinking problem. My cover's been blown. But how? There's no way Annie could have found out who I am, or my connection to Linda's death. Maybe those blokes from the bar turned him in, damn it. He felt trapped.

The voice inside Angus's head was racing. Don't get ahead of yourself mate, you've been in a few tight jams before, you just need to find your way out.

Angus was looking for a way to avoid Annie and the police. In a few minutes time, the boat would be docked. He assumed that he would be arrested as soon as he ascended the gangway. He decided that it was time to abort his mission and get out of town before anything more could go wrong.

He glanced around the harbor for options. At the pier opposite from where the Explorer was docking, lay a fast-looking boat with the name "Wild Thing" emblazoned on its bright yellow hull. Not very subtle, he thought, but it will have to do. He could hear the engine idling as the person whom he presumed was its owner polished the chrome railings.

Angus assessed the situation and realized that his options were slim. Either get that boat and get as far away as possible, or certainly face arrest, and whatever charges came with it.

He felt the Explorer bump against the dock. All of the passengers moved quickly towards the exit ramp en masse. Now was his only chance. Angus quietly made his way to the stern of the ship and, when he was sure no one was looking, slipped over the railing.

Annie waited nervously next to Chief Souza as they watched the passengers disembark.

"Have you seen him yet?"

"No, not yet. There's still a lot of people to go.

"Something doesn't feel right. I'm calling Billy." Chief Souza pulled out his cell phone and pressed Billy's number on his speed dial.

"Billy, it's me. Is the guy still on board?"

"I just saw him a minute ago. I've kind of lost him in the crowd now. Do you want me to check and see if he's hiding anywhere?"

"No, don't do that yet. I don't want to raise any suspicions. Annie and I have been watching the passengers and we haven't seen him yet. There's only one way off the boat. If they all depart and we don't see him, we're coming on board. Keep your eyes open. I don't know who the hell this guy is, but he's sneaky."

Angus only dropped about three feet into the water, but the weight of his clothes and his backpack made it hard for him to reach the surface. When his head broke above the surface of the water, he checked to see if anyone had noticed. Satisfied that they hadn't, Angus moved quietly across the harbor in the gathering darkness.

He approached the stern of the Wild Thing, and called out to the man on board. "Help, help me! I fell overboard!"

When the startled man didn't see him at first, Angus called out again. "Over here! Help me up!" Angus extended his hand as he approached the swim platform of the boat, which he recognized as a Fountain, a fast vessel indeed.

"Oh, my God. Are you all right?"

"Yes, I'm not hurt. Just help me up." Angus extended his left hand to the man while he fished his knife out of his right pocket and opened it with a flick of his thumb.

The man reached out his hand and pulled Angus up onto the deck. His facial expression changed from concern to fear as Angus pressed the point of the blade against his abdomen.

"Don't scream, don't say a word, or I will kill you. Understand?"

The man nodded silently, his eyes wide open in terror.

"Is this your boat?"

He nodded.

"Is there anyone else on board?"

He shook his head no.

"Good. Let's go then."

"Go? Where?"

"I said don't talk." He pressed the blade harder into the man's shirt. "Just untie the boat and get us out of here."

Angus kept a firm grip on the man's arm as he untied the dock lines from the cleats. He kneeled down on the deck next to the man as he put the engines into reverse. Angus kept the knife firm against his ribcage.

"Good, now take us out of the harbor, nice and easy."

The man obliged and pushed the throttles forward. The twin 454 engines rumbled at idle speed. Angus was impressed.

"How much fuel do you have?"

"About 50 gallons." The man answered nervously.

"Is that enough to get to Boston?"

"Yeah, sure. Is that where you want to go?"

"No questions from you mate. Just drive the damn boat."

The Wild Thing rumbled past the Explorer into the fading darkness. Chief Souza saw it moving. He raised his binoculars, and could barely see the top of Angus's head. "That sonofabitch," he muttered.

"What? What do you see?" Annie asked.

"He's getting away. He's hijacked that boat."

"Are you sure?"

"I'm sure." He picked up the microphone to his walkie-talkie. "All units be advised, suspect has commandeered a civilian boat called the Wild Thing. He appears to have a hostage onboard. Dispatch, call the Coast Guard, we'll need their help to catch this guy. They're the only ones with a boat fast enough to catch him."

"Roger that, Chief," Dispatch Officer Thompson responded.

"They're not the only ones," Annie said.

"What do you mean?" He looked down at Annie's outstretched palm and saw her holding the keys to the Whale Center's rescue boat. Their eyes met for a moment, then without hesitation Chief Souza said "Let's go."

Chapter 28

Juicy Freeman lay unconscious at his feet. He felt bad having to hurt him, but the stakes were too high. It wasn't elegant either. He walked up to Juicy and said "Hi", then asked him if he'd seen the blimp hovering over the Pilgrim Monument. Of course, there was no blimp and, when Juicy turned around to look for it, he smacked him in the back of the head with a lead-filled leather blackjack. He waited behind the bushes until he was sure Annie was out of sight.

He retrieved the key from under the stone and let himself into the house, just as he had watched Annie do. He looked around to make sure that no one had seen him, closed the door, and sat down at the computer. Ray Charles hissed at him from the other room, but he had bigger concerns on his mind than an unfriendly house cat.

In order to get the $10,000, he would have to deliver both the report and Annie to Angus Black tonight. He had mixed feelings about bringing Annie into this, and possibly getting her killed, but he saw no other way out. Too much had already gone wrong. If he wanted to stay out of jail he needed to make sure that all of his tracks were covered.

He scrolled through the files on the hard drive and came to the same password protected area that Annie encountered. He didn't see Annie leave with anything in her hands and he hoped that she hadn't printed the report. He looked around to see if he could see any visual clues as to what the password might be. After nearly a dozen unsuccessful tries he gave up.

Knowing that the longer he stayed in the house the greater the risk he had of being caught, he unplugged the laptop computer and put it inside a shopping bag he found in the kitchen. He would take the laptop back to his place where he could spend more time trying to guess the password, and find the file. If he failed, he could just hand over the entire computer to Angus Black and let him deal with it.

The idea struck him that the laptop would be noticed if it were missing, and that his fingerprints could be found where he had touched objects in the house. Not wanting to take any more chances, he decided to make sure that no evidence was left behind.

He found a large candle in the bathroom and a book of matches. He set the candle on a counter in the kitchen and lit the wick. Making sure that all the windows were closed, he turned on each of the four burners on the gas stove after blowing out the pilot lights. He'd never done anything like this before and he wasn't sure how long it would take for the gas to ignite, but he wasted no time getting out the door. As he did, Ray Charles sneaked past his feet and ran out into the garden.

Nine lives, there goes one, he thought.

Nervously, he looked up and down the street to see if anyone was watching him. Satisfied that there were no witnesses other than the cat, he pulled the visor of his cap down low and walked away under a brilliant crimson sky.

Briskly, he made his way towards the center of town. Sweat was trickling down the inside of his shirt as he entered the cool darkness of the Governor Bradford tavern. He made his way to the far end of the bar and ordered a beer. With his head down low so that no one could see his face, he quickly downed the pint and ordered another. By the time he'd finished his second beer, the glasses at the bar rattled with the boom of the explosion. Most of the patrons ran to the window or out into the street to see what had happened, but he remained fixed to his seat, clutching the bag tightly. He saw no point in gawking. The threshold had been crossed. There was no looking back.

Chapter 29

The Wild Thing passed the stone jetty that protects the inner harbor from severe weather. Beyond that was an area where many larger sail and power boats had anchored for the weekend. Angus opened his backpack and removed the Glock pistol that he had sealed in a plastic bag. He was satisfied that it was dry as he slid a loaded clip into the handle.

The boat's driver looked down when he heard the click of the magazine. "Are you going to kill me?" he said with a lump in his throat.

"Not if I don't have to." Angus was genuinely trying to find a way to let this poor sod off the hook. If he were caught, he'd be facing enough charges. He saw two lifejackets under the seat and had an idea. "Put this on."

The man donned the vest and buckled the straps. "Now what?"

"Get out."

"What?"

"Get out of the boat," Angus demanded as he pointed the gun at the man's head. "You can swim to one of those other boats. I really don't want to kill you, but I'm taking your boat. I'll leave it for you in Boston."

Angus watched as the man stepped away from the controls and walked to the stern. Without another word, he turned around and jumped overboard and began swimming toward another boat moored 100 yards away.

Angus tucked the gun into the waistband of his soaking wet trousers and pushed the throttles forward. He was pressed into his seat as nearly 600 horsepower came to life. The sound of the engines was deafening as he headed towards open water at seventy miles per hour.

"C'mon Annie, he's getting away," Chief Souza shouted.

She turned the key in the ignition and both engines immediately started. "Clear the lines!" she yelled.

"Clear!"

Chief Souza threw the ropes onto the dock and nearly lost his footing as Annie slammed the motors into reverse and backed out of the slip.

"Hold on," she said.

The chief turned the VHF radio to channel 16 which the Coast Guard monitored around the clock.

"U.S. Coast Guard, this is Chief Souza, Provincetown Police. We are in pursuit of a speedboat with an armed suspect on board. Can you provide us with backup? Over."

"Roger that, Chief. This is Petty Officer 2nd Class Richmond. We'll certainly help you out. Give me a minute and I'll find out what assets are available. Over."

"Thank you. I'll be standing by."

Annie cleared the breakwater and could see the Wild Thing rounding the tip of Provincetown at Long Point, nearly two miles out. She pushed the throttles all the way forward and felt the boat respond immediately.

"Hopefully the Coast Guard can help us out. That's a really fast boat he's got and he's got quite a lead," Annie said.

"What's that in the water?" the chief asked.

"It's a man. He's waving for help. We've got to stop."

Annie pulled the boat alongside the floating man and Chief Souza reached out to grab hold of his hand and helped pull him on board.

"Are you okay? What happened?" Annie asked him.

"Some nut stole my boat. He pointed a gun at my head and told me to get out and swim. Says he's taking it to Boston."

"So there's no other hostages on board?" Chief Souza asked.

"No. It was just me. I brought my family over for the weekend. My wife and her sister are shopping in town. I was just getting ready to watch the fireworks."

Chief Souza turned his head and looked at Annie. "Hit it. We've got a boat to catch."

She quickly pushed both throttles forward again and they were on the move.

"How fast can that thing go?" she demanded of her new crew mate.

" I've had her up to eighty-five on a flat calm day, but with this chop, he'd be crazy to open her all the way up."

"Unfortunately, this guy's crazy." Chief Souza sighed. "What's your name?"

"Stan Goldman."

"OK, Stan. You're with us now. We've got to catch the man who stole your boat, not just so that you can get it back, but he's wanted on charges of assault and he's now the lead suspect in a murder investigation."

Stan's eyes widened. "OK. Do whatever you need to do."

The VHF radio crackled. "Coast Guard to Provincetown Police Chief, do you copy?"

"Yes, I copy. What have you got for me?"

"Sir, we have a cutter near the east end of Cape Cod Canal, but it will take nearly an hour to get to Provincetown. Do you know the direction the suspect is heading?"

"Apparently, he's trying to get to Boston. Can you head that way and try to intercept?"

"Yes, I'll let the ship know. In the meantime, we've launched a Jayhawk helicopter from Air Station Cape Cod. That's a very fast bird, sir. They ought to be on him in about twenty minutes."

"Very good. Thanks for your assistance. I'll let you know if we need anything else. Out."

"How's a helicopter going to stop him?" Annie asked.

"Ever since the Coast Guard became part of Homeland Security, they've been armed. They didn't used to, but now they carry 50-caliber machine guns, just like the Hueys did back in Vietnam. And they're fast too, they can reach nearly 200 miles per hour. Once they catch up to him, they can force him to stop, one way or another." He paused, "Stan, do you have insurance on that boat?"

He moaned his reply, which Chief Souza took as a no.

"We'll see what we can do," he said, patting Stan on the shoulder.

The trio rounded Long Point and could see the rooster tail wake of the Wild Thing in the distance. Even though they were over

179

a mile away, they could hear the engines screaming.

Chief Souza looked over his shoulder and in the dwindling light could see a column of thick, black smoke rising nearly as high as the Pilgrim Monument. He pressed his radio transmitter button and was instantly connected to the Police Dispatcher.

"Carla, we're in pursuit of the suspect and waiting for Coast Guard backup. I can see smoke coming from town. What's going on?"

"There's a building fire on Commercial Street in the East End. The Dharma Gallery just exploded. All the windows for a block around it are blown out. The fire department is there now, but there's nothing much left."

"That's Mary Ellen's place. What the hell is going on?" Chief shouted over the whine of the motors.

"Oh, my god. I was just there," Annie gasped.

"What do you mean you were just there?"

"Mary Ellen called and asked me to stop in to feed her cat. I did, and then I tried to find the backup copy of the report on Linda's laptop computer."

"Did you?"

"No, it's password protected, and I don't know the password."

"Did you leave the gas on or smell anything burning?"

"No, nothing. I just fed the cat and sat down at the computer. I was only there about twenty minutes before I came to meet you."

"Did anyone follow you?"

"I don't know. Maybe. There was a weird guy outside my apartment just before I went to the gallery."

"I don't know what's going on Annie, but I don't like it. It's not just a coincidence that Linda was killed, and then two days later, her house goes up in flames. Someone's out to cover his tracks."

"I'm scared, Chief, I'll admit that, but right now all I want to do is catch this guy and find out if he's the one behind all of this."

"You and me both."

Angus looked down at his instrument cluster. He was doing a steady seventy-five miles per hour. At this speed, he would be in Boston in about fifty minutes. He was planning to scuttle the boat, get to his car, and leave this whole mess behind, but as he felt confident that he would get away, a red light started blinking next to the oil pressure gauge for the port-side engine.

"Damn it," he shouted.

Turning around, he saw grey smoke pouring out of the engine hatch. Angus watched the needle on the oil pressure gauge drop and the temperature rise. He would have to shut down one engine.

He pulled the left throttle all the way back to cut the power. As he did, he heard a loud blast and saw the engine cover blow off and smoke pour out. The explosion knocked him off his feet. As he fell, Angus gashed his head on a chrome grab handle next to the cabin entrance.

"Bloody hell!" he shouted as he got back onto his feet. He pressed his hand to the wound above his right eye and it came away covered in blood. The other engine was still running, but he knew that his speed would be half of what it had been before, at best. He looked toward the stern, and was relieved to see that there was no fire. What he could see, however, was a boat closing on him at a high rate of speed.

Annie pointed towards the darkening horizon. "Look, there's smoke coming from his boat!"

"What do you think happened?" Chief Souza asked.

"Probably blew an engine driving like a maniac. And that's not his boat, it's mine," Stan reminded Annie.

"He's still moving, but I think we'll catch him," Annie shouted.

"Look, at ten o'clock. Here comes the chopper." Chief Souza pointed to the sky.

Angus saw the helicopter, too. "Uh oh." he muttered. He slammed the throttle all the way forward, pushing his one good engine to its limit. He knew that he couldn't outrun the helicopter and that his best bet was to make it back to land. He turned the wheel hard to the right and held on tight as he spun the boat around to face his pursuers.

"He's turning around. What's he doing?" Annie asked.

"He's trying to scare us. Don't let him, just keep going," Chief Souza ordered as he unholstered his gun.

The two boats closed on each other with a combined speed of nearly eighty miles per hour. From fifty yards away, Angus saw who was chasing him.

He gritted his teeth and snarled, "You stupid little girl. You've no idea who you're messing with." With his gun in hand, he took aim at Annie.

The windshield in front of her shattered as the bullet just missed Annie's head.

"Get down, he's shooting at us!" Chief Souza yelled. Stan

hit the deck as Chief Souza leaned over the side of the boat to return fire. "Annie, are you OK?"

"I'm fine. Don't let him get away."

"I'm not planning on it." Chief Souza fired three times, but all three shots missed.

Angus ducked down, then as he was about to pass the other boat, fired a shot directly at Chief Souza.

The bullet hit him in the shoulder. Annie screamed as she saw Chief Souza drop his gun and fall backwards onto the deck.

As the Wild Thing passed them, Angus kept shooting until his clip was empty. He put his final shots directly into the outboard motors. Both engines immediately stopped running and caught fire. Annie watched with disbelief as the Wild Thing roared by.

"Oh, my god, oh, my god" Stan kept repeating. He was covered in the chief's blood.

Without hesitation, Annie grabbed the VHF radio. "Mayday, Mayday, Mayday, We need help!" she shouted. "A police officer's been shot, and our engines are on fire."

"Copy that, Provincetown PD. We see you. Do you have a life raft?"

Annie looked around and saw the Zodiac lashed to the deck. "Stan, untie that inflatable boat."

He scrambled to his feet and followed her orders as the flames grew higher behind him.

Chief Souza groaned from the deck. "I'm okay Annie, tell them to catch that son of a bitch and come back for me later."

"Like hell, Chief, you've been shot."

"Give me that." He sat up and took the microphone in his good hand. "This is Chief Souza. We are launching a life raft right now. My wounds are only superficial. This suspect is armed and dangerous, don't let him get away."

By this time the helicopter was hovering almost directly over them.

"Roger that, Chief. We have a cutter on the way to your location now. They'll pick you up in about fifteen minutes. Don't worry Chief, this guy's not getting away."

"It's ready," Stan called out.

"Let's go." Annie helped lift Chief Souza to his feet and Stan guided him into the Zodiac. Annie started the outboard motor and as soon as all three were sitting, she revved the engine to put some distance between them and the burning boat. When they were about two hundred feet away, the fuel tanks on the rescue boat exploded sending a huge fireball into the night sky.

The three of them watching in awe as pieces of burning wreckage sank into the ocean.

"Are you really OK, Chief?"

"He just caught the top of my shoulder. I'll live."

"So what are we supposed to do now?" Stan asked.

"Wait for rescue," responded the chief as he gripped his shoulder.

Annie added, "And hope they kill that bastard."

Chapter 30

Angus could barely see the outline of the shore about two miles away. Even with one engine, he could make it to the beach and disappear into the night. He was still moving at nearly forty miles per hour, and would only need a few more minutes to land on the beach.

Angus heard the explosion of the Whale Center boat behind him. He turned around in time to see the fireball rise into the darkening sky. "That's the end of them," he said to himself with the faintest hint of a smile.

As he watched the burning pieces of wreckage sink into the water, he could see the Coast Guard helicopter bearing down on him. In the time he had to recognize what was happening, the Jayhawk's powerful searchlight came on and nearly blinded him. Angus turned back to the boat's controls and pushed the throttle on the one functioning engine all the way forward.

"This is the United States Coast Guard. Stop your vessel immediately," Capt. Robert Cole ordered over the loudspeaker.

"He's not going to stop, who are you kidding?" his co-pilot Lt. Leslie Cunningham said.

"I know, but we have to at least give him a chance to do what's right. Keep the spotlight on him."

Angus maneuvered the boat in an S-like pattern to evade the light. He turned the Wild Thing in a tight 180-degree arc and zipped underneath the helicopter.

"I told you he wasn't going to stop."

Captain Cole spun the helicopter around so that he would not lose sight of the Wild Thing. "Stop your engines now or we will be forced to fire upon you. This is a direct order."

"Fire upon me?" Angus puzzled. "It's the bloody Coast Guard." He drew the handgun out of his waistband and took aim directly at the spotlight. The bullet shattered the light and Angus was plunged into darkness. Satisfied, he turned and continued his run to the beach.

"Sir, he's shooting at us! We've lost our searchlight," Ensign James Martell yelled from the door position.

"Switch to night vision and prepare to fire," Captain Cole ordered.

"Yes sir." Ensign Martell swung the .50 caliber M-60 into position and fed a link of bullets into its firing chamber. All three crewmembers on board flipped down their night vision goggles. Through the green tint, they could clearly see the fleeing Wild Thing. "Ready to fire, sir."

"Put three rounds over his bow. We'll give him one last chance."

"Yes, sir." Ensign Martell pushed a switch on the side of the gun to change the firing setting from automatic to burst. Taking aim through his goggles, he squeezed the trigger once and fired three rounds.

Angus heard the shots and felt the bullets whiz past his head. He didn't know that the U.S. Coast Guard carried heavy weapons on its helicopters, and he quickly reappraised his opinion of them. He whipped around to return fire, but couldn't get a clear sight of the Jayhawk in the night sky.

"He's getting ready to shoot back, sir. What should I do?"

"Take him out, Ensign."

"Yes, sir." With that order, he moved the fire selector to

automatic and put the Wild Thing in his sights. His first twenty rounds hit the water behind the stern, but he then walked the fire up into the engine compartment. The hot lead shredded through the fiberglass hull and tore apart the fuel lines. In a matter of seconds, the Wild Thing's fuel tanks exploded and lit up the night sky.

The helicopter crew hovered overhead, using their night vision goggles to assess if anyone had survived the explosion. There was nothing but a burning hull, and that quickly sank beneath the waves.

"No way anyone lived through that," Lt. Cunningham said grimly.

"Probably not. Just to be sure, we should have the cutter come take a look once they've picked up the others. Let's go home."

"Roger that."

Annie, Stan and Chief Souza watched the firefight in silent awe from their Zodiac. They heard the automatic weapon fire, and saw the explosion light up the underside of the clouds like fireworks. Stan just hung his head and moaned.

"I guess that's the end of him," Chief Souza said quietly while keeping pressure on his wound.

"And my boat," Stan said as he slumped to the floor.

Annie shook her head in disbelief. "I don't get it, Chief. What drives someone to do something like this?"

"Greed, power, hate, lots of reasons. I've seen all of them as motives for murders before, but they come down to the same thing."

"What's that?"

"People who commit crimes feel they're entitled to do

whatever they want without regard for anyone else. They're selfish, selfish to the point where they can't even see the value of a human life."

"So, if Tom Lawrence was just being selfish, what was it that he wanted?"

"Well, if your theory is right that this was all about stopping Linda's report, I'd guess he had financial interests at stake. Who would benefit from the report's suppression?"

It was all making sense to Annie. "The oil companies."

"Right. That's what I've been thinking ever since you mentioned that idea. Do you know of any oil companies that want to move into this area?"

"I do," Stan chimed in. "Some of the Canadian firms are already drilling natural gas off of Nova Scotia. The biggest player up there is Scotia Gas, that's where I'd start looking if I were you."

"How do you know that?" Chief Souza asked with a look of incredulity on his face.

"I'm a fund manager in Boston for New England Securities. We specialize in mid and large cap companies throughout the Northeast and Canada."

"There's good money to be made in that, isn't there?"

"I just watched my $350,000 boat go up in flames, didn't I? It's OK, I'll buy another one."

"Huh." Chief Souza mused about having that kind of disposable income. Some of the gadflies at Town Meeting said that his $90,000 salary wasn't justified. Now here he was bleeding from a bullet wound, in the dark, two miles from shore, waiting to be rescued.

"Here they come." Annie pointed to a searchlight scanning the waters. She and Stan stood up and waved, hoping to be noticed. The beam swung over them, then stopped.

"It's like looking into the sun," Annie said squinting.

"This is the United States Coast Guard Cutter Gosnold. We are dispatching a boat to you. Please remain in your boat." The loudspeaker blared through the darkness.

The three castaways heard an approaching outboard motor, then saw a smaller spotlight approach. In a few minutes, the boat was right along side of them. It looked like a newer version of the Whale Center's rescue boat that had just been sunk.

"Good evening. Is anyone injured?" the boat's medical officer asked.

"He's been shot in the shoulder. We're both OK." Annie shouted back.

"All right, let's get him off first."

"No need to do that. I'll be fine." Chief Souza insisted.

Annie rolled her eyes. "Don't be so stubborn. You've been shot for god's sake."

"You sound like my wife."

"She's right, sir. Come on, now, let's get you out of here." Two young Coast Guardsmen helped Chief Souza to his feet and into the new boat. Once he was seated, the others followed. One of the Coast Guardsmen tied the Zodiac to the stern.

"Let's take a look at you, sir." The medic switched on his flashlight and peeled back the fabric covering the chief's wound. This was the first time Annie actually had a good look at it and the sight made her feel queasy. He was losing far more blood than she'd imagined. The wound wasn't in his shoulder where she thought it was. Rather, the bullet had entered the top part of his chest.

The medic listened with a stethoscope. "Are you having trouble breathing, sir?"

"A little. I'll be all right won't I?" This was the first time Annie heard him express any concern for his situation.

"We need to get you to a hospital right away. I think the bullet may have punctured your right lung." The medic reached for the radio transmitter. "Bring back the Jayhawk. We need a medical evac for a wounded police officer, stat."

"Chief, my god, why didn't you say anything? We could have used the helicopter to get you help."

The chief's breathing became labored. "I didn't want him to get away. It's too important." He reached out and squeezed Annie's hand. "Thanks for your help, sorry about your boat, Stan." As Chief Souza's grip loosened, he closed his eyes and lost consciousness.

Chapter 31

Angus watched the boat speed away from him after he dove overboard. He knew that the explosion would kill him if the bullets didn't do it first. He thought for certain that the helicopter crew would see him in the water and try to finish him off, but to his surprise they did not. Angus treaded water as he watched the Jayhawk turn around and fly away. "First lucky break I've had all bloody day," he muttered.

He could see the lights of Provincetown on the horizon. It was hard to judge the distance, but seeing that his options were limited to a sink or swim decision, he chose the latter.

After nearly an hour in the cold water, he reached the shore just north of Herring Cove Beach. He was thankful for his earlier decision to put on the second life jacket, as he was able to float and rest when he became tired.

He laid shivering on the beach, staring up at the starless sky. He knew his game was up, whether or not his true identity was known. He was, without a doubt, a wanted man. Except for one thing, he realized, "Everyone pursuing me thinks I'm dead."

He could see a small bonfire and a cluster of vehicles a quarter of a mile away down the beach. He stripped off his lifejacket and walked toward the encampment, barefoot, dazed and soaking wet. As he got closer, he saw a row of fishing poles in the sand at the shoreline.

A small group of people were sitting around a campfire. There were two female couples, and three men, all with beer bottles in their hands. Angus smelled a pungent odor that he immediately recognized as marijuana.

He watched from a distance of about thirty yards and saw a bright orange glow rise to the face of each person gathered around the fire. Four cars were parked in the parking lot behind the group. Stealthily, he circled around them, and crept up to the first vehicle, a black Lincoln Navigator with New York license plates. He looked through the open passenger window and saw that the keys had been left in the ignition.

Carefully, he opened the door, slid across the seat, and softly closed the door behind him. He started the engine and put the car into reverse, hoping that the group was too far away and too stoned to hear him. Angus kept a watchful eye on them as he backed the SUV away from the beach, but no one seemed to stir. He shifted the transmission into drive and crept forward, the loudest sound coming from the crunch of the tires on broken shells in the parking lot. When he was sufficiently far away, he turned on the headlights and sped away.

If they think I'm dead, I've got a chance to get away from here, he thought. He didn't like the idea of leaving unfinished business behind, but this entire escapade had gone wrong. What he really wanted was to be at home, soaking in his marble tub, smoking a Cuban cigar and listening to Mozart on his Bose stereo.

Angus had no idea where he was. He was driving through the dunes and forests of the Provincelands, part of the Cape Cod National Seashore. Finally he came to a three way stop. His headlights illuminated a sign pointing to Route 6. The sign indicated that Boston was 149 miles away. He calculated that he could be there in about two hours, leave this car in the parking garage, and head back to Canada in his own vehicle.

He turned left onto Route 6 and drove about a mile when he came to a stop at a red light. Angus looked at the digital clock on the dashboard and realized that it was 9:15 pm. He reasoned that even though his accomplice had proven himself to be inept, there was a chance that he had obtained the Whale Center's report and was waiting for him on his boat. Besides, he was the only one in Provincetown who knew Angus' true identity.

The light turned green, but Angus didn't move. The sign directing him to turn right for Provincetown taunted him. He could get away, and leave a witness behind, or he could take just a few more minutes to ensure that his trail was completely covered.

The gun was lost when he dove overboard. Even if it hadn't been, it would have been useless after an hour in seawater. Angus felt his pocket and found that he still had the knife he'd purchased earlier.

Sweat beaded on Angus' brow. He had made his decision, and his heart started beating faster. He turned right onto Shankpainter Road and drove towards MacMillan Wharf. This was one loose end that had to be cut off.

He found a parking space at the end of the wharf and cautiously walked out towards where the fishing fleet lay at rest. Hundreds of people were gathering on MacMillan Wharf to watch the fireworks. Even though he was wet and barefoot, Angus blended in with the crowd.

He stopped dead in his tracks when he saw a Coast Guard rescue boat dropping two passengers off at the Explorer's dock. "My god, it's Annie. Well, now she's going to get what she deserves," he muttered to himself as he fingered the blade in his pocket. Angus saw a young man embrace Annie as she stepped onto the dock. He held her hand as they walked up the gangway. Angus followed them as they walked down MacMillan Wharf toward the fishing boat slips. The two boarded the Lady J. in darkness.

Angus watched them as they talked on the boat. She was obviously crying, and the man appeared to try to comfort her. Angus smiled, and stalked his prey with confidence.

"I just can't believe what's happened," Shane said as he handed an open beer to Annie. "I was cleaning the boat when I heard what was happening on the VHF. Do you know if the chief's gonna be all right?"

"I don't know. He was bleeding a lot when the helicopter picked him up. He was barely able to get into the basket. I think they're flying him directly to Mass General in Boston." Annie cast her eyes down as she absentmindedly peeled the label off the bottle.

Shane stared out at the harbor for a few minutes before speaking. "I feel so bad about all of this. I never should have left you alone."

"It's not your fault, is it?" Annie snapped. She could see that Shane was taken aback. "I'm sorry. Look, I've been going nonstop since 5:30 this morning. I've been a hostage negotiator, I rescued a whale, I've been shot at. Seriously, Shane, this has not been an easy day."

"I understand. I feel the same way. So, what about the guy who shot the chief, is he dead?"

"I hope so. I just can't believe that all this happened because of oil money."

"There's a lot of cash in oil, Annie. Better than lobstering, that's for damn sure."

Annie looked puzzled. "What do you mean? I thought you loved lobstering."

"Oh, come on, Annie, let's face it, the fishing industry is on it's last legs here. I bust my hump ten, sometimes twelve hours a day," he shouted. "For what? By the time I've paid for diesel, maintenance on the boat, licenses, and everything else, I'm lucky to make $25,000 a year. That doesn't go far these days." He spun around and threw his bottle angrily toward the harbor.

"Shane, what's the matter with you? You're scaring me."

"Annie, I know this guy from Nova Scotia. I met him at a conference I went to in college. He said that after the fishing industry collapsed in Canada, oil and gas was all they had left. Those are good jobs, with benefits, pensions, everything a fisherman's never going to see."

"So, you think they should open up George's Bank to oil exploration? I can't believe what I'm hearing."

"Keep talking, lad. You're making good sense," Angus said as he appeared out of the shadows. He walked down the ramp to the Lady J and stepped on board.

Annie was too much in shock to scream. She looked at Angus' bruised and swollen face, his wet clothes, and shook her head in disbelief. "I, I thought you were dead," she stammered.

"I hope you're not disappointed, Annie," Angus said with a sinister chuckle.

"Shane, do you know him? What the hell is going on?"

"Annie, this is the guy I was telling you about."

Annie lunged towards Angus. "You sonofabitch, you killed Linda!"

Angus grabbed her arms, spun her around and threw her to the deck. "Not me, love, I had nothing to do with her. Why don't you ask your boyfriend here about what happened?"

Annie looked up at Shane with a look of disbelief and fear. "Shane, tell me it's not true. He's lying, right? It's not true, is it?"

Shane couldn't make eye contact with her. "I'm sorry, Annie. It wasn't supposed to work out this way."

The first volley of fireworks exploded above their heads, as the Provincetown skyline lit up in flashes of red and purple.

"No, it wasn't, was it?" Angus roared. "This was supposed to be really simple. You see, love, your boy here was supposed to get me the report that Dr. Hanscomb and you were working on, but he messed up, and she got killed. I was ready to give him a job as my local contact here. But now, well, plans have changed a bit, eh?" Angus pulled the knife out of his pocket and flicked open the blade. Shane's eyes widened in shock as Angus plunged the knife into his abdomen. He screamed out in pain and slouched to the deck next to Annie.

Annie's scream was drowned out by the next burst of fireworks. She tried to scramble out of his path, but there was nowhere to go. She had been backed into a corner and Angus was walking toward her with Shane's blood dripping off the knife in his hand.

Annie reached frantically for something, anything, which she could use to defend herself, but her hands came up empty. Out of the corner of her eye, she saw the silhouette of a large man jumping from the pier onto the deck of the Lady J.

Annie watched in complete shock as Johnny Souza, the Chief's estranged brother, swung a long handled object at Angus. The gaff hook embedded itself deep into Angus's right shoulder. He screamed in pain and dropped the knife. Johnny yanked Angus off his feet with the tuna gaff and Angus crashed hard onto the deck. With fireworks illuminating the boat, Annie scrambled to her feet and went to check to see if Shane was still alive.

He looked up into her eyes. "Annie. I am so sorry. I didn't want this to happen."

"Sorry doesn't even begin to cut it." Annie clenched her fist and punched him as hard as she could in the face. "You lied to me, you said you loved me, and you killed one of the nicest, most compassionate people I've ever known. Did you know she was pregnant? Did you? You're nothing, Shane, a nobody. I can't believe I fell for you." Shane dropped his head and began to sob.

Johnny Souza pinned Angus to the deck of the Lady J with the heel of his boot. "Who the hell do you think you are? You shot my brother. We might have our differences, but he's a good man. You don't mess with my family. I'm gonna see to it that you pay." He turned to Annie and said, "Miss, throw me that rope."

Annie tossed him a piece of black nylon rope that was lying on the deck. She now recognized that it was the same rope used to tie Linda's hands and feet. Johnny Souza lashed Angus's hands behind his back, and with one hand picked him up by the back of his shirt.

"What are you going to do, kill me?" Angus moaned.

Annie could see flashing blue and red lights approaching as three police cars and an ambulance made their way through the crowd on MacMillan Wharf. They came to a stop at the end of the ramp to the commercial pier, and six officers ran to the Lady J with their guns drawn.

"That would be too easy. No, I'm going to let you rot in a jail cell for the rest of your pathetic life."

"Nobody move. You, drop what you're holding," one of the cops commanded Johnny. He let the tuna gaff drop to the deck.

"These are the guys you want. This is the one who shot Chief Souza, and this is the rotten, lying, bastard who killed Linda Hanscomb." She said pointing to Shane. "They'll both need ambulances. I wouldn't want them to miss their trials."

"Nice work, Miss," Officer Silva said as he handcuffed Shane and yanked him to his feet.

Annie watched as Shane and Angus were led away to the ambulance. "Is there any word on Chief Souza?" she asked the officers.

"He was still alive when they got to the hospital. They took him into surgery. That's the last I heard," Officer Silva said.

Johnny gently laid his weathered hand on her shoulder. "He'll be O.K. He's a fighter. We Portuguese are pretty tough."

"Damn right we are," Captain Billy Souza said as he walked down the ramp to the boat. "Thanks, Uncle John. I don't know what would have happened if you weren't here."

Billy put one arm around Annie's shoulder. "Are you O.K.?"

On MacMillan Wharf, crowds of people clapped and shouted as the deafening finale of fireworks echoed over Cape Cod Bay.

"No," was all that Annie could manage to say. Annie turned into his open arms, hugged his broad shoulders and let the trauma of the day flow out of her in tears.

Chapter 32

Annie found it hard to believe that six months had passed since that horrible summer weekend. As she fidgeted with her jewelry, she reviewed in her mind all that had happened since. Shane was found guilty of first degree murder and was sentenced to life without parole. Angus Black was being held indefinitely under the Patriot Act at an undisclosed location. His shooting at a United States Coast Guard helicopter qualified him as an enemy combatant.

"How do I look?" Annie asked Mary Ellen.

"Beautiful, but here, wear this, it was Linda's and I want you to have it." Mary Ellen pulled a silver pin of a mother and calf humpback whale out of her pocket. She fastened it carefully to the black pinstripe suit jacket that Annie wore. "You're doing this in her name. I know she'd be proud of you." Mary Ellen gave her a quick hug and a kiss on the cheek.

"Thanks. I think I'm ready now." After Linda's funeral, Bruce Waters asked her to present the report to the Senate Subcommittee on Ocean Affairs on behalf of the Whale Center. She was honored to be asked, and accepted without hesitation. He also offered her the position of Associate Director upon her graduation, provided that she enroll in a Ph.D. program in Marine Biology.

Billy Souza held the door for her as she entered the U.S. Senate Chamber. She wore with pride the diamond engagement ring that he gave her on New Years Eve. Billy leaned in to give her a kiss.

"I love you." he said.

"I love you too." Billy had been kind to her throughout Shane's trial and conviction. He supported her unconditionally. She admired his gentle strength and his integrity. By early September, they were both smitten with each other.

"Now go give 'em hell. Just like Linda would have."

Annie walked through the door and entered the enormous hall. She sat at a table draped with blue fabric facing the panel of seven Senators.

"Ms. Macalister," Senator Carl Bowen, the subcommittee chair and a Republican from South Carolina, began. "On behalf of the Senate Subcommittee on Ocean Affairs, we welcome you to this hearing. Before us is a very serious issue, that being the matter of oil and gas drilling in the Gulf of Maine. We have heard from representatives of the oil industry who are of the opinion that oil and gas extraction would be of tremendous social, economic, and strategic benefit for the New England States, and indeed the entire nation. I understand that you have a different opinion, and we invite you to tell us about it."

Annie shifted in her seat. She could feel the support of Mary Ellen, Billy, Bruce, Chief Souza, and her parents, behind her. She cleared her throat and began to read her opening statement which suddenly sounded too much like a term paper to her. She glanced up from her notes, looked directly into the eyes of the panel of white haired men, and spoke into the microphone.

"Thank you Senator, and thanks to all of you for being willing to hear another side to this story. I do, in fact, have a different opinion regarding this issue. For over two hundred years the migratory whales which feed in the Gulf of Maine have been threatened by human activity. All of the species of great whales, humpbacks, finbacks, sperm whales, and right whales, were hunted nearly to extinction. Some have recovered their populations, some have not. The North Atlantic Right Whale has a total population of around 300 individuals. That's fewer people than are in this room. Imagine, if you will, that there were only that many human beings left in the world, and someone from another planet wanted to build an industrial complex in the middle of the only place where they can eat and nurse their young."

"Are you saying that this is the only place in the world that they feed?" Senator Doherty from Maine asked.

"Yes Senator, I am. They go to the Caribbean in the fall and winter months to give birth to their calves, but there is virtually no food in those warmer waters. The Right Whales migrate up the coast in the early spring and arrive in the Gulf of Maine in April or May. The cold water holds lots of plankton that they need to eat. As the summer goes on, they migrate further north up into Canadian waters."

Senator Bowen drawled, "Frankly, I don't see how drilling platforms and ships are going to do any harm. The oil companies told us yesterday that they'll take every precaution to ensure that no whales are injured. Whales are supposed to be pretty smart after all, they'll just swim around them."

"With all due respect, Senator, I have some personal experience with the oil companies. I really don't think that they have the interests of anyone or anything other than their own profits in mind."

"Would you please share with us your experience?" Senator Flynn from Massachusetts urged.

Annie launched into the story about Angus Black, and how Scotia Gas was under investigation for corruption and fraud in both U.S. and Canadian courts. She told how Angus arranged for the break-in that led to Linda's death. The entire panel sat back in their seats and listened carefully as she recounted how she nearly became a victim as well.

"So, to conclude. Allowing for oil and gas exploration in the Gulf of Maine is a clear violation of the Endangered Species Act and the Marine Mammal Protection Act. It poses a tremendous threat to the most endangered species of whale in the world, all for the extraction of an unknown amount of petroleum. I urge this committee to consider the survival of a species over the profits of a corporation. Thank you for allowing me the opportunity to address you."

"Thank you very much, Ms. Macalister," Senator Bowen said. "We've heard both sides now. The subcommittee will take a short recess, and when we return, we will have a vote on whether or not to extend the current moratorium on petroleum exploration in the Gulf of Maine." He banged the gavel on the table to signify the recess.

"Great job, Annie. Linda would be proud." Bruce Waters patted her on the back.

"Now, I understand just what this is all about. I'm so proud of you," Annie's stepfather whispered in her ear.

She smiled and said, "Thanks."

"Well, what do you think?" Annie asked Billy.

"You did a great job, but they're a tough bunch. Two of those senators are from oil states. There's no way they'll give in. The rest, we'll just have to wait and see."

Senator Bowen banged the gavel again to bring the room back to order. It was obvious that he enjoyed the power this gave him.

"Ladies and gentlemen, we're back in session now. I would like to thank all of those who participated for their testimony. This is certainly not an easy issue to resolve. I believe we're ready for a vote, who would like to call the motion?"

"I will," Senator Flynn from Massachusetts spoke. "I move to re-authorize and extend the moratorium on oil and gas drilling in the Gulf of Maine for another twenty-five years, as in the provisions of the current law."

"Second." Senator Doherty from Maine said.

"All in favor?" Senator Bowen asked. Senators Flynn, Doherty, Capistrano and Johnston raised their hands in unison and voted, "Aye!"

"All opposed?" Senators Bowen, Anderson and Floyd raised their hands and groaned, "Nay."

The room erupted in applause. Annie watched with her mouth open as a line of dark suited lawyers and oil industry lobbyists slinked down the aisle to the exit door.

Senator Bowen banged his gavel one last time and announced, "this hearing is hereby adjourned."

"What does that mean? Did we win?" Annie excitedly asked Bruce.

"Yes, we won. You won!" He hugged her shoulders. "And you even won over Johnston, a republican from Georgia."

Annie put her hands over her mouth. She wanted to cheer, but instead all she was able to do was cry. Billy wrapped his arms around her and whispered in her ear, "I knew you could do it. I always did."

"It wasn't me. It was Linda."

ABOUT THE AUTHOR

Richard Gifford lives on Cape Cod with his wife Nancy and their two sons Benjamin and Jack. As a native Cape Codder, he is drawn to the oceans, the beaches and the people who make the Cape such a special place.